The door
follow
Audrey bringing up the rear.

"So what's the verdict?" Jenna asked.

"Our killer just doesn't care what we find," Dr. Slikowski declared grimly. "The savagery was not an attempt to hide the stragulation. But finding the strangulation, and amidst that savagery, we did almost miss a vital clue."

"Anyone else *would* have missed it," Dyson added.

"On the girl's skin we found twin burn marks. Electrocution. It wasn't the cause of death, but it's the key to this particular murder," the M.E. said.

Jenna was confused. "How's that?"

But Danny had already caught on. "Taser?" he asked.

Audrey nodded.

"So now we know how the killer got Stephanie Tyll off the street without any noise or struggle," Danny said. "Which leaves open the possibility that you're right. Psych profiles would say that the killings are too vicious to be a woman.

"But it's still *very* possible."

Available from Pocket Books

christopher golden

SOUL SURVIVOR

A *Body of Evidence* thriller starring Jenna Blake

POCKET PULSE

New York   London   Toronto   Sydney   Singapore

An *Original* Publication of POCKET BOOKS

 POCKET PULSE published by
Pocket Books, a division of Simon & Schuster Inc.
1230 Avenue of the Americas, New York, NY 10020

ISBN: 0-671-03494-4

First Pocket Pulse printing November 1999

10 9 8 7 6 5 4 3 2 1

POCKET PULSE and colophon are trademarks of
Simon & Schuster Inc.

Front cover illustration by Kamil Vojnar

Printed in the U.S.A.

for José Nieto and Steve Eliopoulos

acknowledgments

Thanks, as always, to Connie and the boys; to my agent, Lori Perkins; and to my editor, Lisa Clancy, as well as to her team supreme, Liz Shiflett and Micol Ostow. Also, a big thanks to Allie Costa and Cat Morgillo and to the regular crew: Tom, Bob, Stefan, and Jeff. Special thanks this time around to Dr. Jennifer Keates (you did it!).

acknowledgments

Thanks to Sheila, Connie, and Pat Scott Connor
again, Mark Dressler, and to my editor, Lisa Clancy, as
well as former team upstairs, Liz Stein and Alisa
Davis. Also, a big thanks to Allie, Carol and Cal
Kraft; and to the resident genius Rob, Bob, Amir,
and all Spend Clark 52, and Amanda in Los Angeles.
Peace, I am out. bit.

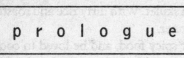

prologue

It was the day before Halloween, and Bill Broderick felt invincible. With the full moon shining above, he jogged along the paved path that ran beside the Charles River, on the Cambridge side, and let the adrenaline take hold.

Bill was pumped. Not just from the run, but from the day he'd had. Before he'd finished his coffee that morning, he'd managed to get Shawna Mallette to agree to go to dinner Halloween night. By two o'clock he'd scored a million-dollar client for Constellation Software. Half an hour later the district manager had called him in to congratulate him, and to let him know that a management slot would be opening up and he was in contention for it.

At three-thirty, afraid to give such a perfect day any chance of blemish, Bill had told his secretary to call him on the cell phone if there was anything urgent. He'd then headed for his fifth-floor two-bedroom overlooking the Charles. He'd listened to messages, caught up on e-mail, and then cooked himself some blackened chicken in a cast-iron skillet. With dirty rice and roasted peppers, that was dinner.

Bill had a taste for spicy food, and he loved to cook. He only wished his stomach was as cast-iron as the pan.

After dinner he'd made a quick call to a client in La Jolla—still early in California—and then changed into sweats. With his portable CD player pumping Joan Osborne's early recordings through the mini headphones, he'd headed out for a run.

It was chilly, but not bad for the end of October. Even the breeze off the river didn't really cut through his Boston College sweatshirt. The moon was full, and it shimmered on the river. *Pretty sweet*, Bill thought. You couldn't tell how dirty the Charles was after dark.

Yeah, he felt invincible.

The blood pumped through his veins, the music thrummed in his ears, and his heart beat in time with his feet on the pavement. The path wound in among the trees between river and road, and Bill reminded himself how brilliant an idea it had been to move here. The new apartment was close to Harvard Square, but right on the Charles. There was always something going on, and if it was something on the river, whether it was a concert or the Head of the Charles regatta, he could see it from his small balcony.

Never mind the women who studied or sunned

themselves in Charles River Park on every sunny day from April to September.

Which brought Bill back to Shawna. He still couldn't believe that she'd agreed to dinner. They'd worked together for months, and though they always got along well, she'd blown off his advances completely. And why not? He was a notorious dog. Though he didn't talk too much about his social life around her, he did plenty of bragging around the other guys in the office. All bucking to be the alpha male, of course. But there could only ever be one alpha male in any given situation. Bill wasn't one hundred percent confident that he was it, but he was damned sure he wasn't going to let anyone else take the title without a fight.

Still, in spite of his self-inflicted reputation for not exactly being the most sensitive of guys, Shawna had actually agreed to go out with him. Bill hadn't done a great job covering up his surprise, and she'd laughed at the look on his face.

"Don't be so stunned," she'd said. "I figure once you get past the arrogant exterior, maybe there's some raw clay that could be molded into a decent guy."

Bill had smiled. "Don't get your hopes up."

Now it was his hopes that were up.

He ran, working up a good sweat, heart working, reminding him his body was a machine. That's what he always thought about when he exercised. A machine needed tending. He nodded in time with Joan Osborne and wondered how right Shawna might be. Sure, he was kind of a dog. But he was always honest with women, never lied to them. He thought of himself as a pretty decent guy, in spite of the fact that he never seemed to be able to stick it out with someone past the first few months.

Time would tell . . .

Bill grunted. Started to slow. The CD was between songs, and in that moment of silence he thought he heard something. The next song started up, slow and sultry, but he reached up and pulled the headphones off.

A woman screamed.

With a low curse under his breath, his mind working furiously, Bill left the path without hesitation. The rest of the path was well lit, but two lights were out here, and the river water looked black as he ran toward it . . . toward the bridge that went over the Charles and into Boston, with only the full moon to guide him.

There, at the base of the bridge, far from the path, he saw her. There was an expression on the woman's face as she ran from under the bridge, a look of fear unlike anything Bill had seen before. He had put his own fears aside, rushing to the aid of a stranger on instinct, despite the darkness, despite the unknown. But now, as she ran toward him, not so much running as desperately flailing, he felt the first tingle of fright begin to creep up inside him, calming the lightning reflex that had prompted him to go to her aid.

But then she was there . . .

"Oh, thank God," she huffed, throwing herself into his arms. "He's . . . oh, if you hadn't come."

If she hadn't seemed so grateful, so reliant upon him, he might have left then. Just walked away with her, helped her to the police station, something like that. Something practical. But something within him heard the plaintive tone of her voice, and he stood a little taller. Bill was angry with the bastard who'd attacked this woman. This *beautiful* woman. He hadn't noticed that at first, but she was beautiful indeed. Dark and exotic. Perhaps forty, more than ten years his senior, she was nevertheless striking. She wore a long, crimson silk scarf around her neck.

Then she said the words.

"Please don't let him get away."

Bill stared at her, into her soulful eyes. "Don't worry," he said.

And he ran for the blackness beneath the bridge. He could hear the cars rumbling above, and the soft, swift running of the river, but from the dark, he heard nothing.

Though he'd been coming from a darkened path, the night somehow seemed more solid down here, out of sight of the moon. It took a moment for his eyes to adjust. The lights of the city across the river, mute witness to the scene unfolding there on the bank, were all that he had to see by. But it was enough.

Bill blinked. He wanted to make certain his brain was correctly processing what he was seeing there. On the stone foundation of the bridge, in white spray paint that picked up the light from the city, were horrible images. *A man with the head of an elephant. A figure with four*

5

arms dancing on a corpse. An orb—perhaps the moon—but with the features of a skull.

And on the ground, in a wide spot that had been cleared of the sort of debris that littered the rest of that dark space, Bill saw a shopping bag on its side. Most of its contents seemed to have been laid out there on the ground: a skull, a glass jar of what might have been sand, a long knife, and several dark objects just inside the bag.

"What the hell is this?" Bill asked himself aloud.

There was no one there to hear him. Though he hadn't heard anyone running off as he approached, the woman's attacker must have escaped out to the path on the other side of the foundation. He'd be long gone by now. But just looking at the things he'd left behind, Bill realized just how lucky the woman had been. *Better get the police down here,* he thought. *This guy is a complete nutjob. They've gotta get him before he hurts someone.*

Bill started to back up. Though he heard nothing, he sensed someone was behind him and began to turn. He was too late. A flash of red slipped past his eyes and then he was being strangled, his air cut off completely. He knew he had to react, to thrash, to drop to the ground—something—but in the instant of hesitation and shock, he was driven forward, headfirst, into the stone foundation of the bridge.

The impact broke his nose and cut his forehead. And he fell. He was quickly running out of air, the oblivion of unconsciousness slipping over him. He tried to force his body to rise up, but it would not obey his commands.

In the last moment of thought he had left to him, he felt the soft, tender kiss of a woman's lips. Smelled her sweet perfume. And she spoke.

"You were so brave."

Then he knew that the thing around his neck, stealing his life, was a scarf made of crimson silk . . .

He was dead. That was good. But the face had been damaged. Still, it would be all right. It would heal, if all went well. She took a thick, black marker from the bag and on his forehead she drew a third eye, above and between the ones he had been born with.

She had to drag him, just a little, so that the light of the full moon fell across his face. With her gloved hands, she opened the jar and sprinkled ashes over his body, then threw both jar and marker into the river. She knelt by the dead man for several moments, staring into his lifeless eyes, staring into the third eye she had drawn, and willing it to open, praying that it would open.

Then she lifted the skull in both hands, and with it, she began to dance.

c h a p t e r   1

In the common area on the third floor of Sparrow Hall, Jenna Blake sat on a hideous beer-stained orange chair and stared at Caitlyn Janssen in abject horror.

"You're actually going to do it?" Jenna asked, astonished. Then she glanced over at her roommate, Yoshiko Kitsuta, just to confirm that she wasn't nuts, that Yoshiko was getting this too. "They're actually going to do it?"

"Yeah," Caitlyn scoffed. "I mean, why the hell not?"

Jenna didn't have an answer for that. She never would have imagined she would need an answer for that.

"Well," Yoshiko ventured, "there's the whole naked thing, for starters."

"Oh, come on, Yoshiko," Olivia Adams said, her tone almost condescending. "You've got nothing to be ashamed of. You're in great shape. And it isn't like you'd be alone out there. Half the people in Sparrow are going."

"Yeah, the wacky half," Jenna muttered.

"Okay, hey!" Olivia snapped.

"Sorry," Jenna said, and shrugged. "You guys want to go run around the quad buck naked with a bunch of spectators cheering you on—and getting an eyeful—that's up to you."

"It's a tradition," Caitlyn said, blowing a long strand of her stylishly clipped blond hair out of her eyes. "Every Halloween, the residents of Sparrow run around the quad naked. Sure, it's embarrassing—"

Yoshiko snorted. "Never mind cold."

"But it's all in good fun. Plus you guys are, like, the only people on this floor who aren't going to be out there."

Jenna laughed. "Now you're just being crazy," she said. "I think you're getting cold feet, and you want us to come to give you courage or whatever. I know plenty of people who aren't running. Sam and Brad, that's two. Laura."

"Hunter," Yoshiko added.

"Huh?" Olivia frowned. "Hunter's running. I just saw him not ten minutes ago in Keith Belinksy's room. He's going."

Yoshiko blinked. Jenna raised her eyebrows, and then a small smile started to creep across her features. The four of them sat there in the common area in complete silence for a moment. Then Jenna laughed, and Yoshiko chuckled a little and brought one hand up to her forehead, as though feeling for a fever.

"Well, now we really can't run," Jenna said. "Being naked in front of a whole bunch of people isn't my idea of a good time. And I'm not clear on whether *anyone's* ever seen Yoshiko naked."

Her roommate glared daggers at her, but she was smiling.

"But sitting on the sidelines watching all of you guys—particularly Hunter—run around the quad in the nude?" Jenna continued. "Now that's my idea of a good time. Especially if we have squirt guns."

"Don't you dare!" Caitlyn said, aghast.

"Oh, I'll dare," Jenna laughed. "I'm brave that way. The no-clothes thing, no bravery there. But taunting and torturing others for fun and profit, oh yeah. Call me Daredevil."

Yoshiko still seemed a little thunderstruck by the revelation that Hunter was going to be joining the run. Jenna didn't blame her. Not only had Hunter fed them some ridiculous line about how silly he thought the whole thing was, but he'd actually concocted an excuse to be out of the dorm at the time of the run, so they wouldn't know he was going to be out there. He was obviously afraid they would heckle him.

And he's right, Jenna thought.

Not only was he their friend, but he was also sort of Yoshiko's semi-boyfriend. What had started as friendship was quickly becoming something else, and Jenna was all for it.

Mostly.

There were complications that she hadn't envisioned

11

when she first supported the idea of the pairing. Most of them stemmed from one, horrible tragedy, which they were all doing their best to put behind them. A month earlier, Hunter's sister Melody, who had also been Jenna's best friend, had been murdered right there on campus. The killer, a nondescript man named Jarrod Coffey, had been caught partially because of Jenna's involvement.

But that didn't stop her grief. It didn't stop her from being haunted. The pain was something the three of them shared, but as Yoshiko and Hunter grew closer, Jenna had begun to feel, more and more, as though she were dealing with it on her own. She played it off as if it didn't matter, because she felt as if that was what was expected of her. But really, it did matter. She wished she felt as though she could talk to them more about it. At the same time, she didn't want to make it any more difficult for Hunter than she knew it must be.

In the wake of Melody's murder, Jenna had focused more on her classwork, and on her job. There hadn't been a great deal of *social* in her social life lately. So this, tonight, was a welcome change. She and Yoshiko had started to hang around the dorm with Caitlyn and Olivia, who lived a few doors down. The girls were as different as Jenna and Yoshiko, which made the foursome pretty fun and interesting.

Caitlyn was from Highland Park, Illinois, which Jenna got the idea was a pretty wealthy area. She was rushing AOPi, hoping to become a pledge at the sorority, mainly because her mother had been an AOPi when she had attended Somerset.

Olivia, on the other hand, was from Philadelphia, and very active with the Somerset African-American League. The SAAL was always hosting one charitable fund-raiser or another, working with the community, but there was something about it Jenna didn't get. While one of the group's goals was to foster understanding among the diverse races on campus, nearly all of their events were for members only. And since one had to be African-American to become a member, Jenna didn't see how much understanding that could foster.

Fortunately, Olivia was very open-minded and very willing to discuss and debate just about anything, and the four of them had had some very interesting discussions on race, politics, religion, sex, and just about anything else they could think of.

They were friends, the four of them, but they weren't close friends. With Melody's death, there were only a handful of students on campus Jenna felt close to. Yoshiko. Hunter. And then there was . . .

"Hey, Damon," Caitlyn said brightly.

The girls all looked up to see Damon Harris coming down the hall with two other guys. Damon lived on the third floor as well, and he and Jenna had gone out a few times, though it hadn't come to anything. They'd remained friends, though, and gotten closer over the past few weeks—a lot of late-night study sessions and talks. He was a good guy all-around, and devastatingly handsome. Sometimes she wondered why they'd never followed through on their initial mutual interest.

Jenna recognized his friends, too. They didn't live in Sparrow, but she knew them because Damon seemed to spend all his time with them. The one on the left was Anthony. He was broad-chested and quiet and played football for the Somerset Colts.

The other guy was called Brick, but though she'd never heard him called anything else, Jenna didn't think that was his real name. Brick was heavy into the theater scene at Somerset. In fact, he'd been cast as Captain Von Trapp in their production of *The Sound of Music*, before the show had been canceled. Melody was supposed to play Maria in the show, but after her murder, they simply canceled it. Brick had been sweet to Jenna after that, and she liked him for it.

"What are you guys doing here?" Olivia demanded sharply, as Damon and his buddies walked over.

"Getting naked," Damon replied happily. "And I hope that's what you all are doing too."

When he spoke, his eyes flickered over to Jenna and he smiled, teasing. They'd talked about it earlier, and he knew she had no intention of going out there.

"You guys don't live in Sparrow," Olivia added, glaring at Anthony and Brick.

Anthony shrugged, a small smile on his face.

"I'm more a doer than a bystander," Brick told her.

They all sort of laughed at that.

"So you're really going to do it?" Jenna asked Damon.

He smiled. "Just close your eyes when I go by, will you? I'm starting to feel a little shy."

Jenna chuckled and shook her head. Damon beamed at her, and then the three guys walked on down to the guys' end of the third floor. As soon as they were gone, Yoshiko turned to Jenna with a questioning glance.

"Are you sure you two are just friends?" she asked.

The smile left Jenna's face. "Huh? Yeah. Of course. I mean, we hang out, but that's it."

"Don't be so sure," Caitlyn said coyly.

"What's that supposed to mean?" Jenna asked, frowning.

"I don't know," the other girl replied. "You guys have kind of a current going on. Definitely charged atoms flying through the air around here."

Jenna glanced away, almost blushing. "I'm not seeing it."

"No," Yoshiko allowed, "but don't tell me you're not feeling it."

"Can we talk about being naked in public some more?" Jenna asked impatiently.

"Actually, we should go," Caitlyn said, standing up and looking at Olivia. "I mean, if we're gonna get naked, it's almost time."

"Yeah," Olivia said noncommittally.

She was looking at Jenna oddly, almost frowning. Jenna felt awkward for a moment as she tried to figure out if she'd said something wrong. Then it hit her that Olivia might have a thing for Damon, and their talking had made her jealous.

You can have him, Jenna thought. They really were

only friends. Mostly. And even if there was some lingering attraction there, it wasn't anything that would get in the way of Olivia's getting to know him better.

Whatever, Jenna thought.

"Okay, guys, well, we'll see you," Yoshiko said gleefully as the other two girls got up and headed off to their room.

"Work that double entendre, roomie," Jenna told Yoshiko.

All in all, and in spite of Olivia's weirdness, Jenna was more relaxed, more content, than she'd been since Melody's murder. Just hanging out, having a good time, that was what she needed so desperately.

"So, what do you think? Should we get our squirt guns?" Jenna asked.

"Well, at the very least we should mock them as they pass," Yoshiko replied. "That is, if my workaholic roomie can stand to blow off studying for an entire night."

"I think I'll manage."

"And on a Tuesday night, no less," Yoshiko marveled.

"Hey, I finished my Rasputin paper an entire week early," Jenna said proudly. "I deserve a break. I deserve to taunt those foolish enough to run the nudie gauntlet."

"And admire some of them," Yoshiko reminded her.

"Like your boyfriend?" Jenna asked.

"He's not my boyfriend. Exactly. Yet. And *you* keep your eyes shut," Yoshiko warned.

16

"How will I tease him, then?" Jenna asked, wide-eyed with feigned innocence.

"You'll find a way."

Jenna did actually own a squirt gun, but in the end, they couldn't find it. She figured it must have been borrowed by someone on the floor and never returned. That was college life. Her favorite hairbrush had walked off in just the same way.

Not having a squirt gun didn't make the infamous "Sparrow Hall Halloween Run" any less entertaining. It was cold outside, maybe forty-five degrees, and there were plenty of lights on the broad span of lawn that stretched between several of the uphill dormitories. And yet, to Jenna and Yoshiko's open-mouthed astonishment and raucous laughter, at a few minutes past nine o'clock, the doors to Sparrow Hall swung open, and dozens of students, most clad only in socks and sneakers, ran out and started around the quad in front of several hundred people who had gathered to watch and cheer.

In the lead was Jack Counihan, a junior who was also one of Sparrow's resident assistants. Tonight he was assisting by setting the pace for the jog. Not too fast. Not too slow.

Jenna's eyes were wide, and she felt her cheeks flush a little as people she knew or at least recognized went past her. It wasn't that far around the quad, only a few minutes to jog, but Jenna couldn't imagine how long those few minutes would have seemed if she'd been one of the joggers.

"Look!" Yoshiko said, and nudged her.

Caitlyn and Olivia ran by, laughing and waving at the friends and strangers who were cheering. Jenna and Yoshiko screamed and laughed and waved back.

"Oh my God," Jenna said as the other girls moved on, "I can't believe they really did it."

"Maybe I'll have the guts next year," Yoshiko said. "If we're back in Sparrow."

Jenna gave her a dubious look.

"What? It could happen."

"So could world peace, but I'm not holding my breath," Jenna said.

But Yoshiko wasn't listening. Jenna saw that her roommate's eyes were focused somewhere else, and turned to look back at the runners going by. Then she saw Damon.

Jenna clapped both hands to her face and peeked through her fingers.

Damon saw her, grinned, and held up one finger in a shame-on-you gesture that had Jenna doubled over laughing and blushing deep red. When she looked up, her roommate was smirking at her.

"Just friends, huh?" Yoshiko said.

"Yes," Jenna insisted. "Unlike certain other people we know."

Yoshiko smiled even before she looked up and saw Hunter. He was jogging behind Sam Chin, and the two of them had big, silly grins on their faces. Jenna took one look at Hunter, and couldn't help laughing. He was very pale, and skinny, and had on black sneakers and bright orange socks, apparently in honor of Halloween.

"You're not supposed to look," Yoshiko reminded her, only half serious.

Jenna did more than look.

"Yay, Hunter!" she screamed. "Nice booty, LaChance!"

Yoshiko whacked her on the arm, but it was too late. Hunter had spotted them. He looked horrified, flushed red from his chest on up, and tried desperately to cover himself up as he ran past. After a moment's hesitation, he moved next to Sam, who was even thinner than he was, and tried to use him as camouflage.

Jenna kept hooting, and after a minute, so did Yoshiko. This would give them both ammunition against Hunter for a long time. After Hunter had passed, there were only half a dozen more students. When they'd gone by, Yoshiko looked at Jenna and frowned.

"Nice booty?" she asked doubtfully.

"A little bony, actually," Jenna told her.

"Hey!"

Yoshiko chased her back into the dorm, actually beating Hunter inside. They took the north-side stairs, what was technically the girls' side. Though the males had outnumbered the females during the run by about four to one, there were still a number of girls coming in from outside and sprinting up the stairs to get back to their rooms and put their clothes on. *Slightly odd sensation,* Jenna thought. *Walking fully clothed up the stairs next to a bunch of naked people.*

But it wasn't until she and Yoshiko got into their

19

room and closed the door that they turned to each other and started to laugh. They giggled over how insane the whole thing had been, but mostly about the look on Hunter's face when he had seen them.

Twenty minutes later, while they were sitting together watching an ancient rerun of *Seinfeld*, there was a knock at the door. When Jenna opened the door to see Hunter standing in the hall, unable to meet her gaze, she and Yoshiko both broke out in another fit of the giggles.

After a few seconds, though, Hunter grew impatient. "It's not *that* funny!" he insisted.

"I guess that all depends on your perspective," Jenna said. Before he could become further offended, though, she held up a hand to forestall an argument and to calm herself down. "I've got to say, Hunter, I'm pretty impressed that you came right over here."

She turned to Yoshiko. "He's got courage. Not afraid to face the music."

Yoshiko smiled and went over to Hunter. "Not afraid of much, other than our torment," she said, and kissed him lightly on the lips.

Hunter blinked, a little surprised. He wasn't the only one. Though Jenna knew they were becoming involved, it wasn't like Yoshiko to be so openly affectionate. Of course, things were progressing with them, and it wasn't as if Jenna didn't know. She'd thought it sort of weird that things had been moving as slowly as they had.

Hunter kissed Yoshiko back, and then she apparently

reached her limit, because she gave him a little push away, smiled, and then just held his hand.

"Ah, get a room," Jenna teased.

"Why bother?" Hunter asked. "I've got no secrets from either of you now."

"Some things are better kept secret," Jenna replied.

They both laughed, but Jenna felt in some way as though the laugh didn't extend to her, didn't include her. It was an odd feeling, though one she was having more and more frequently around them. A couple thing. *A third wheel thing.* She tried to shake it off, was even about to make a joke of it, when she saw the look that Hunter was giving Yoshiko.

A look that was just for Yoshiko. "Brad and Sam are giving a free beer to anyone who did the run," Hunter said. "Do you want to socialize, or are you planning to hibernate in here tonight?"

"No beer for me," Yoshiko replied, "but socialization works."

Jenna didn't respond to Hunter's question because she knew it wasn't really meant for her. She just sat, leaning against her bottom bunk, and watched *Seinfeld.* After a moment, though, Yoshiko turned toward her.

"You coming with?" she asked.

"I'm wallflowering," Jenna replied. "I think I'm going to get some sleep. I'm afraid I've had a little too much excitement for one night."

When she said that last, she raised her eyebrows suggestively. Hunter blushed again and Yoshiko chuckled. Then, after Yoshiko checked her appearance in the mirror above the sink between their closets, they went out into the hallway, closing the door behind them.

Jenna wasn't very good at sulking. It hadn't been something she'd been in the habit of doing, even as a kid. But as she crawled into bed, she felt as though she was sulking, and she was angry at herself for it.

You could go out there, Blake, she told herself. *Hunter and Yoshiko are there. Damon and his friends. Sam and Brad. Caitlyn and Olivia. You have friends.*

But she missed the kind of friendship she'd had with Melody, and that she sort of had with Hunter and Yoshiko, when they weren't so wrapped up in each other. Her two best friends from high school, Moira and Priya, were good about keeping in touch by e-mail, but they'd all been slacking lately on that front. Too much to do, she supposed. And her father was just as preoccupied. He was a professor at Somerset. Not only was he struggling to complete a book, dealing with the publish-or-perish imperative of academic life, but he'd recently begun dating Shayna Emerson, an English professor Jenna had been pushing him to ask out for ages.

Jenna just needed someone to talk to.

At least, that was what she kept telling herself. But as she curled up and closed her eyes, *Seinfeld* still on, volume low, television light flickering across the room, Jenna realized a hard truth: she might be lonely, she might feel left out, but it wasn't just that she needed someone to talk to.

I need Melody *to talk to. And she's never coming back.*

chapter 2

When her alarm went off early the next morning, Jenna winced and purposely kept her eyes shut for a few seconds. With a sigh, she reached out and switched it off, then turned to look out the window. November was not starting out with any promise. It was a gray day, like she imagined nuclear winter would be. Which about summed up how much she was dreading crawling out of her bed.

Yoshiko wasn't around, and Jenna knew she was probably already in the shower. Her roommate was always more punctual than she was, and took more care with her appearance this early in the morning.

At length, she reminded herself that Professor Lebo hated when students were late to class, and she dragged herself up and went down the hall, half-asleep, to take a shower. When she came back, freshly scrubbed, Yoshiko was already dressed, slipping into a new pair of leather shoes she'd bought the week before.

"Hey," Yoshiko said brightly. "I guess we must have crossed paths in the bathroom."

Jenna blinked, still a bit sleepy but getting over it. "How can you be so up this morning?" she asked. "Haven't you looked outside?"

Yoshiko smiled. "Jenna, I grew up in Hawaii. I re signed myself to the weather in New England the first week of school."

"Yeah, well, give me Hawaii any day." Jenna sighed.

"Do you want to have lunch later at Nadel?" Yoshiko asked.

"Can't. I'm meeting my dad at the campus center. Come down if you want, though," she offered.

"Maybe," Yoshiko replied noncommittally.

She left while Jenna was still trying to figure out what to wear. She had to work later, and that pretty much ruled out sweatpants, which was how she felt today. In the end, she went with black jeans and a turtleneck under an olive green fleece top. She usually dressed a little less casually for work.

I just don't have the brain mojo workin' this morning.

She grabbed her black leather jacket from her closet, and she was out the door.

Somehow, though the building where her biology class was held was just across the quad from Sparrow, she still managed to be late. Professor Lebo raised an eyebrow and shot Jenna a withering glance as she walked in, but she had only just begun her lecture. Plus, Jenna knew her a little bit outside of class, since she had once needed to consult with her on a work-related matter. She didn't think the professor would give her too much of a hard time.

Unless she made it a habit.

Halfway through class, though, Jenna scored even more points in the negative column by nodding off slightly. Her head was bobbing and there didn't seem to be anything she could do about it. Finally, she noticed Professor Lebo staring at her, and that sat her up straight and wide-eyed. Still, the damage had been done.

Way to stay on her good side, Jenna chided herself.

Fortunately, Spanish class went a little better. She managed to stay awake, and actually felt as though she had gotten the hang of the language. Not that she'd ever be fluent. She didn't plan on pursuing it that far. But she was in the groove somehow, and it made learning and studying that much easier.

When it was over, she headed downhill to the Campus Center to meet her father for lunch. Jenna and her dad, Frank Logan, had been getting to know each other—in some ways for the first time—since she had come to Somerset, where he was a professor. Her parents had divorced when she was very young, and for a long time, she saw her father only a few times a year, sometimes less. Getting acquainted had been a learning experience, but she was enjoying it.

They tried to make it a point to get together at least a couple times a week, even just to watch a movie and have popcorn in his living room. It was nice for her, having him around, particularly because he worried about her and gave her advice but realized that he couldn't really *parent* her.

Lately, though, he'd seemed a little distant. As a condition of his tenure, he was under pressure to publish another book in his field, which was law and criminology, and the writing was apparently not coming easily for him. And now that he was dating Shayna, Jenna had to compete with her for her dad's attention.

But today I've got him all to myself.

Forty minutes after she arrived at the Campus Center, Jenna had to accept the fact that he wasn't coming. She'd called his apartment several times and received no answer. Finally, she'd left him a curt message indicating that she hoped there was an emergency somewhere, otherwise he'd get a severe dose of venomous sarcasm.

As she wolfed down a tuna sandwich, and then rushed off to her international relations class, she realized that she wasn't really angry with him. Just sad.

By the time Jenna's IR class let out, a bit of blue had started to break through the gray. It had even warmed up a little, and she stopped by her room to put the leather back in her closet. Between the turtleneck and the fleece, she was plenty warm.

Of course the sun comes out just in time for me to go to work.

Actually, though, Jenna found the idea of going in to work to be rather comforting, as perverse as that would seem to people who didn't really understand. As a pathology assistant at Somerset Medical Center—a teaching hospital that was part of the larger complex that included Somerset's undergraduate and medical schools—Jenna worked for Dr. Walter Slikowski, the county medical examiner. She did paperwork. Updated computer records. Answered the phone. Transcribed recordings.

And sometimes—more frequently than she ever would have imagined—she assisted at autopsies.

More importantly, at least to her, she and Dr. Slikowski had established an excellent working relationship. He was more than just the M.E., he was also a forensic consultant for law enforcement officials all over the county, sometimes the state, and on rare occasions, the nation.

As part of that relationship, Jenna had actually helped to solve certain crimes. It brought her closer to Dr. Slikowski, who seemed to see in her a mind as inquisitive and as persistent as his own when it came to solving puzzles. Jenna had quickly realized after taking the position that every death they dealt with was a kind of puzzle. That element of it appealed to her profoundly.

All in all, it was a pretty cool job.

So what if people don't get the whole hanging-with-dead-bodies thing. After all, it wasn't as if *that* was the part of the job she liked. Actually, she'd started to think of herself as lucky to have found something so early on that she enjoyed and that she knew she was good at. Or could be good at. In fact, a part of her had started to think of Dr. Slikowski as kind of like Batman, and herself as his Robin.

Or maybe Batgirl. But not the Alicia version.

Contemplating all of this helped to pull her out of the funk she'd been in since the night before As Jenna crossed Carpenter Street and headed along the path that took her past the medical school and SMC itself, she smiled in anticipation.

Work was good.

Moments later, she rode the elevator up to the administrative wing on the second floor of Somerset Medical Center, and walked down to Dr. Slikowski's office. The door was open. When Jenna walked in, she nearly collided with Dr. Albert Dyson, SMC's pathology resident, who assisted the M.E. and often performed the autopsies himself when his always-in-demand boss was not available.

"Whoa!" Dyson said, stopping short, then taking a deep breath. "What's your hurry, Jenna? Give a guy a heart attack, why don't you?"

"You kidding?" Jenna replied, grinning. "I've been trying. I don't think I could give a guy a toothache."

"Well then, you're not going after the right guys," Dyson said sweetly, combing back his tightly curled hair with his hands and giving her the goofiest of grins.

Jenna rolled her eyes. "Please!"

He was only fooling around, of course. There was no real flirtation between them, and Jenna wasn't attracted to Dyson anyway. But she liked him a great deal. In truth, before she got to know Dr. Slikowski a little better, Dyson had been her saving grace. The medical examiner could seem a little distant sometimes.

All right, most of the time.

"I just finished writing you a note," Dyson told her. "We've got a weird one downstairs. And I—"

"Know how much Jenna likes the weird ones," she finished for him, sighing. "That's a misconception, Dyson. I like to figure out the whys and wherefores, not necessarily get hip-deep in the gory hows."

Despite her protests, however, Jenna followed him back out into the hall and waited while he locked the door.

"That's the job, J," Dyson said as they walked down the hall to the elevator. "Besides, Slick asked specifically for you to come down. I think he has a surprise for you."

Jenna screwed up her face into an expression that was half smile and half terror. "You realize that doesn't do a hell of a lot for me. A surprise from a guy who spends his days cutting up corpses?"

"You spend several afternoons a week watching us cut up corpses," Dyson replied.

The elevator door opened, and they stepped in. Jenna punched the button for the basement.

"Got me there," Jenna told him. "Maybe it's my own scalpel, y'know? With my initials engraved in it and all?"

Dyson looked askance at her. "Don't get all crazy, kid."

Jenna punched him lightly in the arm. "I've told you not to call me that," she said.

"Ow!" Dyson whined. "When did you ever—"

"Just now," Jenna snapped, and glared at him playfully.

Rubbing his shoulder, Dyson faced front with an expression of mock gravity on his face. "I shall have to speak with Dr. Slikowski about your behavior, young lady," he said. "Honestly, it's beyond me why he puts up with your childish and completely unprofessional antics."

"Oh, look who's talking!" Jenna cried.

Dyson's serious face cracked into a small smile, and Jenna punched him again for his trouble. He turned on her, looking pretty devious, and she was wondering if he was going to hit her back when the elevator doors opened. Jenna looked up to see Tony Xin, an orderly she knew, looking in at them dubiously.

"Hello, Jenna. Dr. Dyson," Tony said as they stepped off. "Everything all right?"

"Hi, Tony," Jenna said pleasantly, and walked on past him.

"Xena over there was just brutalizing me," Dyson told Tony.

The orderly laughed, holding open the elevator door. "Yeah. She's a tough one, all right. Listen, I helped Dr. Slikowski get your cold one up on the table, and I think he was planning to start without you."

Jenna paused and glanced back at them, surprised. Slick didn't usually begin an autopsy without at least someone there to assist. Dyson only nodded, and then hurried to catch up with Jenna.

"What's the rush?" Jenna asked.

"No idea," Dyson admitted.

But all the lightness had gone out of his tone. Jenna's curiosity was piqued, and obviously Dyson's was as well. As they walked together, Jenna thought about Dyson, and wondered why she'd never thought about talking to him about how sad she'd been. Over the past two months, they had developed a kind of older brother–younger sister relationship that she had begun to cherish. But it was only in the workplace. She never really confided anything of her inner life to him.

Something held her back. She wondered if maybe it was a kind of implicit understanding between the two of them, some knowledge that their work together set the boundaries of their friendship. Sort of like the people she sat with and talked to in some of her classes, but never even thought to make plans with for outside of class.

Still, she was glad she had Dyson around just on general principle. He always made her smile. Even now, as they walked past the entrance to the morgue and on down to the door to the autopsy room.

Dyson didn't knock. He turned the knob and opened the door, letting out a rush of smooth jazz piano that Jenna immediately recognized as the work of Marcus Roberts. Working with Slick, who lived and breathed the stuff, she had come to know some of his favorites.

Together, Jenna and Dyson walked into the strangest

and most fascinating and most disturbing place she'd ever been. It got less so over time, sort of like the burning sensation in her eyes and nostrils from the stink of formaldehyde. But also like that smell, it never quite went away.

The autopsy room was, to Jenna's mind, something like a futuristic film where everything was stark and cold and metal, with the camera and instruments that hung around the autopsy table, and the stainless steel shelving units and sinks. In his wheelchair, with a body tilted toward him on the specially designed autopsy table, Slick seemed to be a part of that twisted metal world.

Pay no attention to that man behind the curtain, Jenna thought suddenly. The idea of Slick as the Great and Powerful Oz struck her as more odd than funny, and she frowned.

Jazz flooded from the speakers of the sound system that Slick had finally installed at Jenna's suggestion. He'd thought it somewhat improper until she successfully argued that no one ever came into the autopsy room except for hospital staff and law enforcement. But since then, Jenna had wished she'd kept her mouth shut. It was a bit disconcerting hearing the alternately sweet and sad music play while they did what they did.

Fortunately, he could never play it very loud during the actual autopsy. Otherwise the music would drown out his voice while he made his notes on tape for later transcription.

A moment after they'd entered, Slick drew a scalpel

along the chest of the man on the table, creating a
Y-shaped incision she knew he could have made with his
eyes closed. The face of a dead person always seemed to
look older, and Jenna had learned to adjust her age estimates accordingly. She figured the victim for early thirties.
And *victim* was the word, all right. That much was immediately evident thanks to the bruises and lacerations on his
face.

Jenna frowned as she noticed that someone had
drawn a circle or something on the dead guy's forehead
with black Magic Marker. *Weird.*

"Walter?" Dyson ventured.

Slick looked up at them and nodded once without
speaking. He wheeled backward and set the scalpel
down on a metal tray. Then he reached up and pulled
down the cloth mask that covered his nose and mouth.
He was a thin man with a birdlike face and wire-
rimmed glasses. His hair was a salt-and-pepper gray
that made him look older and sort of distinguished,
Jenna thought.

"You're both here," he said. "Good." Then he smiled
a bit, and tilted his head slightly to look at Jenna. "What
do you see?" he asked.

Jenna blinked. "Sorry, but huh?"

Slick waved a hand, gesturing to the corpse on the
table. Somewhere Marcus Roberts ended and the CD
changer kicked in, and a moment later, Wynton
Marsalis started blatting away on his horn, distracting
her. Jenna kind of liked Wynton Marsalis, but not
enough to go out and buy it. Not yet, anyway.

"You mean him?" she asked, then felt stupid. Jenna glanced around awkwardly a moment, wondering why Slick was putting her on the spot. Then she stepped over and opened a cabinet door, pulling out a cap and gown, as well as a pair of gloves and a mask. After she'd put them on, she walked back to the autopsy table and bent over the dead man to get a closer look.

"Well," she said at length, "besides the mess that's been made of his face, I'd say from a quick look he's been strangled. Ligature marks on his neck, there." She pointed, glanced up at Slick, but his expression didn't change.

Behind her, Dyson was slipping on a gown, but Jenna sensed that he was watching her, probably just as curious about what Slick was up to as she was.

"Is this some kind of secret pathology initiation?" she asked. " 'Cause, y'know, nobody told me."

"Go on," Slick urged her.

Jenna narrowed her gaze as she looked at her boss. "Well, we can't make snap judgments, right? I mean, no determining cause of death until the autopsy is over. But I'd guess we'll find fibers on his throat, maybe a crushed larynx."

That seemed to satisfy him, and Dr. Slikowski nodded as Dyson went around to the other side and prepared to crack the victim's ribs to get to the organs. Slick turned the volume down on the CD player, and clicked on the tape recorder where it hung from a cord above the table.

"Subject, William Broderick; autopsy 712-093-46,"

he began. "Caucasian male. Age twenty-eight. Height, five feet nine inches, weight, one hundred eighty-six pounds."

He went on like that for a bit, and Dyson began to remove the internal organs. Jenna had seen the basic autopsy a couple of dozen times now, and she had it down. She knew she should be over with Dyson, helping him weigh and dissect the organs and label samples for the lab. But something about the corpse in front of her had caught her attention.

Something was odd.

After a minute or two Slick paused and clicked off the tape. Jenna looked up to find him looking at her curiously.

"What is it?" he asked.

"I've only seen one other strangulation victim," she began.

Slick nodded. "Domestic abuse victim. Alyson Martin. Three weeks ago. No relation to this crime, though."

"No," Jenna said, by way of agreement. "That woman was killed by her husband. This guy . . ."

"Go on," Slick urged.

Jenna shrugged. "I'm probably wrong. It even feels stupid. But the way the ligature marks are, the way they kind of curve back and down on the sides of his neck . . . whoever strangled him must have been a few inches shorter than he was. He isn't that tall to begin with, so we're either talking a really short guy, or a woman."

"Not likely to find a woman strong enough to strangle a man to death. This guy had some muscle on him, too," Dyson said.

"Come on, Al, you know the rules," Slick chided Dyson. "We deal in what is possible, not probable."

Dyson shrugged. "Okay, possible."

"I've said it before, Jenna, and I'll say it again. You have an excellent eye for detail," the M.E. told her. Then he turned to Dyson. "Al, do you mind finishing up on your own?"

"Of course not. You have an appointment?" Dyson asked.

Slick looked back to Jenna. "The Cambridge police have asked me to visit the crime scene on this one, see if I can't give them some input as to what might have happened there.

"And Jenna's going to come with me."

So that's the surprise, Jenna thought. *I could've just done with chocolate.*

Then, after it had sunk in a bit, she realized that it was somewhat exciting. Dr. Slikowski had sort of taken her under his wing these past few weeks, ever since she'd been the one to make the breakthrough in logic that helped identify Melody's murderer.

"Hey, field trip," Dyson pointed out, looking at Jenna. "Not bad. Of course, nobody ever asks the resident on a field trip."

Slick raised an eyebrow and looked at Dyson over the wire rims of his glasses. "You hate this kind of thing, Dr. Dyson. I've heard it from your own lips dozens of times. You're a clinician, a pathologist first, last, and always."

He wheeled back from the table and pulled off his mask and gloves, then began to glide around toward the front of the room, where Jenna still stood.

"Our Miss Blake, on the other hand, is of a more investigatory bent. The forensic end of things never fails to garner her interest," the M.E. said, and he looked at her. "What do you say, Jenna? Shall we see if we can't help the Cambridge police out a bit?"

"I'm up for it," Jenna agreed.

"Oh my," Dyson said, his voice taking on a kind of weepy quality.

Jenna looked up to see him pretending to dab at his eyes.

"Our little one's first crime scene," Dyson said. "Look at her. She's all grown up."

Even Slick chuckled at that one. Jenna made a face at Dyson, who just grinned. Then Dr. Slikowski led the way out of the autopsy room, leaving Dyson to finish up. Slick had sort of half broken his cardinal rule never to determine cause of death before the autopsy was finished. But Dyson would find anything they hadn't counted on, and Slick certainly wouldn't make any ruling until the two of them discussed it. Still, it seemed a bit maverick of him.

Maybe I'm rubbing off, Jenna thought, and a mischievous little smile crossed her lips.

As they rode the elevator up to the lobby, she was surprised to find herself growing even more excited in anticipation of the short trip they had to make to Cambridge. In the past, all the puzzles she had helped to solve, or watched Slick and Dyson solve, had been done in the sterile environment of the autopsy room or the office. This was something else entirely.

The medical examiner's office put together only a section of the puzzle with each case that came through their doors. This time, Jenna would get to see a bit more of the puzzle than she ever had before.

The experience would prove to be far from pleasant.

chapter 3

Slick listened to jazz in the car, too.

Well, van, actually. There was a lot of traffic as the M.E. drove through Somerset and into Cambridge. But Jenna barely paid attention to the delays, or to Cassandra Wilson on the CD player. She'd never been in Dr. Slikowski's van before, and she was fascinated by it.

He had a special hydraulic lift that extended from the open side door to the ground. Slick wheeled his chair onto the platform, and it lifted him up and withdrew into the van. Once inside, his upper body was strong enough to pull himself into the driver's seat. This was the first time that she'd realized that his legs weren't completely useless. Dr. Slikowski couldn't walk, but his legs could support him, at least momentarily.

Jenna was even more fascinated when he got behind the wheel. It had occurred to her to wonder how he managed to drive, but just as she'd never asked him why he couldn't walk, she certainly never inquired about driving. Now she learned that the van had been equipped so that he could operate the brake and accelerator using instruments attached to the steering wheel.

While they were stopped at a light just outside Harvard Square, Slick caught her looking.

"That's . . . pretty cool," she said, trying to cover her embarrassment. "Was it hard to learn to drive like that?"

Slick smiled. "The most difficult thing was training myself not to tap my hands along with the music while I'm driving."

Jenna chuckled, and suddenly felt somehow more comfortable with her boss than she ever had before. The light changed, and then they were cruising through Harvard Square to get out to Memorial Drive. As usual, the Square was filled with people, a cross section of humanity, but with a preponderance of college students. Pedestrians crossed the street in streams, and Dr. Slikowski had to slow several times.

As they passed the building that housed The Million Year Picnic, a comic-book store Hunter had dragged her into a few times, Slick turned to glance at her again.

"We haven't spoken very much about things unrelated to work, Jenna," he said earnestly. "But how *are* you?"

It was a moment before Jenna replied. She didn't need to ask what he was talking about. Both Slick and Dyson were aware of how shaken she'd been by

Melody's murder. Jenna and Dyson had talked about it quite a bit, but Slick hadn't brought it up since that whole nightmare had come to its violent conclusion.

"I'm all right," she told him.

"It's not difficult for you, doing this work after what you've been through?" he asked, guiding the car toward the Charles River, then turning left to drive alongside it.

"Are you serious? Work's about the only thing that keeps my mind *off* it," Jenna told him. "Sort of ironic, I guess."

"Well, if you'd like to talk about it at some point, you only need to ask," he told her.

Jenna was touched. It wasn't like Slick, at least in her experience, to reach out on a personal level. Between this conversation, and the fact that she was here with him at all, she felt better than she had in a while. While everyone else back at Somerset was preparing for life after college, Jenna was getting her college education without waiting for life to start. Here it was, unfolding before her.

And it's pretty intense.

Up ahead, Jenna spotted a police cruiser, roof lights flashing, pulled over onto the curb. In front of it was a second car, a drab-looking sedan that was conspicuous by its very plainness. It might as well have had "unmarked police car" printed on the doors, as far as Jenna was concerned.

Dr. Slikowski clicked on the left turn signal and pulled in carefully in front of the unmarked car, bumping up over the curb as he did so. A moment later, it made for a somewhat awkward exit from the van, as the hydraulic lift was tilted slightly backward; but there were no mishaps.

Jenna stood next to the lift, waiting for her boss. As Slick was lowering to the ground in his chair, an older, uniformed cop got out of the cruiser and walked over to them. He took one look at Jenna and frowned, a smirk on his face.

"Hey, Doc, what's this?" the officer asked. "Nobody told me it was Take Your Daughter to Work Day."

Then he laughed.

Jenna blinked, hurt and angry but trying not to show it. She glared at the cop for an eyeblink, then turned to look at Dr. Slikowski, as the platform settled at a slight angle to the grass.

Slick had a deep frown on his face. He was staring at the cop.

"Miss Blake is my assistant, Officer . . ." he said, and paused, looking at the cop with a puzzled expression. "I'm sorry, I can't seem to remember your name."

The cop looked offended, and Jenna stifled the urge to grin. Dr. Slikowski consulted with a lot of the local police departments, but most frequently with Cambridge, Somerset, and Boston. More than likely, he'd met the obnoxious officer on many occasions. It wasn't like Slick to be rude, but he obviously wasn't going to let anyone get away with treating one of his people poorly.

Jenna liked that.

Taught that condescending jerk a lesson, she thought.

Even though she realized that the officer probably had no idea he'd offended anyone.

"I see Detective Flannery's car," the M.E. went on, pretending not to notice the officer's annoyance. "He's expecting me."

"Yeah. He told me," the cop grunted. Then he turned and pointed along the grassy park that ran beside the river, toward one of the bridges that spanned the Charles, connecting Cambridge to Boston. "Right down there."

"Thank you," Slick said.

He started to push his wheelchair off the platform and onto the grass. Jenna wondered if he would have any trouble, but it seemed to take him very little effort, and a few seconds later, he was on the paved path that wound through the narrow park. Dr. Slikowski was stronger than he looked.

She glanced at the cop and smiled pleasantly. "You'll be around, right?" she asked, nodding toward the van, the side of which was still wide open, the platform down. "We shouldn't be long, and it'll be easier if we can just leave this open."

The cop sighed in annoyance. "I'll be here."

"Thanks," Jenna replied, giving him her most charming smile.

He smiled back. "No problem." She actually thought the smile was genuine, which was good. No matter how annoying he might be, Jenna thought it best to stay on the good side of the police.

She set off after Slick. As she walked, she focused on

the bridge. There was a stretch of land maybe twenty feet wide between its foundations and the edge of the river. It was very dark under there, even with the sun coming out, and that was where the M.E. was headed.

Jenna caught up to Dr. Slikowski, and thought about saying something about their exchange with the officer. Then she thought better of it. It wasn't the kind of thing he seemed comfortable talking about, despite his offer in the car. She also didn't ask him if she should push his chair. From experience, she knew that he preferred to move under his own power whenever possible.

As they came within a few yards of the bridge, a man appeared suddenly from the alcove beneath it, and Jenna immediately assumed he was Detective Flannery. He was a large man, with thinning gray hair and a bushy mustache. Flannery wore a gray suit with a red tie that seemed, instead of hanging from his neck, to be draped over his considerable belly.

"Hey, Walt, thanks for coming," Flannery said grimly.

"Joe," Dr. Slikowski replied. "What can I do for you?"

Detective Flannery glanced at Jenna and gave her the once-over. He looked curious and doubtful, and then he put voice to his doubts.

"I know you still teach a little over at Somerset, Walt, but I don't know that a crime scene is the place for a field trip."

This time Jenna didn't give Slick time to defend her. "This isn't a field trip, Detective," she said icily. "I am a student at Somerset. You got that right. But I'm also a pathology assistant at SMC, and as such, I work with Dr. Slikowski. If you'd rather I weren't here—"

"You're fortunate to have Jenna here," Slick interrupted. "She's a very astute and observant young woman. Be careful, Joe. If you're not polite, you may have to answer to her one day when I'm put out to pasture."

Flannery laughed at that and held up both hands in surrender. "Whoa!" he said. "Give a guy a break. Misunderstanding, that's all. Nice to meet you, Jenna. I'm looking for all the help I can get. This is a weird one, no doubt."

"Well, let's have a look," Slick said, and started to wheel himself forward, following Flannery under the bridge.

For a moment Jenna just stared after them. Despite Flannery's quick pseudoapology, she was still pretty pissed off about the attitude she'd gotten from both him and the uniformed officer. For the most part, she hadn't dealt with Somerset cops besides Danny Mariano and his partner, Audrey Gaines. They knew her through her job, so they accepted her as part of the team. Now she was beginning to wonder if other cops there would act the way these guys had.

She'd been so excited when Slick asked her to come along. But now Jenna realized for the first time that there were going to be a lot of people doubting her ability to do her job, never mind the job she might one day aspire to, just because of her age or her gender.

Which sucks. But I'm not going to let that stop me.

Maybe the cops would snub her. Fine. But Slick believed in her. Hell, half a minute ago, he'd practically told Flannery he expected Jenna to have his job someday. She knew that he was kidding, making a point, but the fact that he would say it at all gave her a huge lift.

"Jenna?" Slick called from under the bridge. "Are you coming?"

"Oh, yeah," she said, nodding, and then followed them into the shadows.

Police tape was strung from tall wooden stakes that jutted from the ground. Within the imperfect rectangle the tape had created, Jenna could see the spray-painted outline where the corpse had been found. But the instant she saw that, her eyes were drawn to the foundation of the bridge, where someone else had used spray paint to create some pretty disturbing images. One of them seemed to be an elephant man or something. Another was an eerie-looking skull face, but Jenna thought it was too round to be just a skull. Then she had it. The moon.

The worst was the third and largest of the images. A human figure with four arms standing or walking over what looked like a dead man. As Slick and Flannery talked, Jenna's eyes kept going back to those images.

"Did you find the marker?" Slick asked.

"Nah. We figure the guy threw it in the river. And nobody's diving the Charles looking for a Magic Marker."

At the word *guy,* Jenna tore her gaze away from the wall to focus on the two men. Dr. Slikowski didn't seem inclined to argue the point, so she kept silent. Maybe she was way off base, and it was only a guess really, but Slick seemed to have agreed with her back at SMC that it could be a woman.

"Do you think the killer painted these?" she asked, indicating the images on the wall.

Flannery nodded. "It's possible," he said. "With that mark on his forehead, it looks like something ritual. Maybe. We're trying to figure out what they're supposed to mean, see if we can find any connection to the crime. The dancing figure there is apparently supposed to be Shiva."

Jenna looked confused. "Someone I should know?"

"An Indian deity," Slick told her.

"That's him. Anyway, we're looking into it," Flannery said. "But to be honest, that's not my biggest mystery right now."

"What would that be?" the M.E. asked.

Flannery walked over to the stone wall of the foundation and pointed to a dry, brown smear that Jenna suddenly realized must be blood.

"Figure he got that head wound and broken nose over here, and there were some signs of a struggle on the ground," the detective explained.

Then he turned and walked out from under the bridge. Jenna and Dr. Slikowski followed him. Jenna was glad to be out of there. *Too freaky,* she thought, and shuddered. It felt safer out in the open, with so many buildings in sight, both in Cambridge across the road, and in Boston on the other side of the river. She knew it wasn't safer, of course. It just felt that way.

All of a sudden, she understood what had happened, even before Flannery spoke.

"Guy was jogging," the detective said. "Did it regularly. Was wearing sweats, had a portable disc player with headphones, all that. From what we know, the late Bill Broderick was a smart guy. So why'd he go from the path, down under the bridge?

"If somebody overpowered him on the path and dragged him down there, I don't know that we'd have the signs of a struggle we've got under the bridge. Never mind the risk the perp would have taken jumping the guy out in the open. You've got to figure Broderick went down there without a struggle. I can't figure it out."

Jenna was nodding to herself. She glanced over at Slick and saw that he'd removed his glasses and was wiping them on his shirt. He slipped them back on, then met Jenna's gaze and offered a thin smile.

"It appears your theory was correct," he said.

"Huh?" Flannery grunted. "What theory might that be?"

Jenna was enjoying the attention, but she didn't let it show. Instead, she looked very thoughtful, and walked over to the path where Broderick must have been running the night of his murder. She turned and looked back toward the men.

"Damsel in distress syndrome," she said with sympathy. "Most men have it, Detective Flannery."

For a moment the man appeared befuddled. Then he blinked in surprise as he realized what she was suggesting. Then he scowled in dismissal.

"You're telling me you think a woman did this?" he said doubtfully. "I'm not saying it's impossible. But think about it. Woman commits a murder, it's almost always a domestic situation. You just don't get that many female predators out there. Secondly, Broderick wasn't a big guy, but you've got to be pretty strong to strangle a man to death."

"Maybe so," Jenna replied. Then she explained about the angle of the ligature marks on the corpse, and reminded Flannery that Broderick was probably disoriented after receiving the head wound.

"You buy all this?" he asked Slick.

Dr. Slikowski's face was neutral. "It's quite possible," he said. "You shouldn't discount it outright, Joe."

But the detective *wasn't* buying it—not for a minute.

"Yeah," he said reluctantly. "I'll keep that in mind. Thanks for comin' down, anyway. Give me a call if you come up with anything."

Jenna started to get a kind of sick feeling in the pit of her stomach. She'd had it earlier, when they'd dismissed her so readily. Now she was even more perturbed, but she said nothing. She worked for Dr. Slikowski, and he expected her to behave professionally. No matter how angry she was, that was what she planned to do.

"Certainly," Slick said, and then began wheeling himself toward the van. Toward the officer who stood by his cruiser, watching them come.

They'll probably have a good laugh when we're gone. Maybe the take-your-daughter-to-work-day joke will come up again. That one was a riot.

Jenna kept silent.

They reached the van, and Dr. Slikowski spun his wheelchair around, and then backed it up onto the angled platform. He toggled the switch to make it rise. As it was lifting him up, he cleared his throat slightly.

"Joe, is your lab running tests on the ash found on the body?" he asked.

The detective frowned. "I'm not sure what you mean. There was sand and dirt and—"

"Not sand," Slick corrected. "Ash. And apparently not. I'm going to send a sample to the lab. I'll let you know what they find."

Suddenly, Joe Flannery's expression changed. Jenna thought she could read it pretty well, actually. Her presence had thrown off the usual dynamic between these men. Flannery had sort of misplaced his knowledge of Dr. Slikowski's reputation and expertise and past cooperation with the Cambridge P.D. Now he remembered it well enough to appreciate it.

"Great," Flannery said. "And thanks, Walt."

"Don't mention it," Slick replied. But his tone with Flannery was nowhere near as friendly as it had been when they'd arrived.

After they'd pulled away from the curb, Dr. Slikowski turned and smiled at Jenna.

"Gold star, Jenna," he said. "You handled them very well."

"Yeah," she scoffed. "I'm a pro. Are you kidding? They totally blew me off. What the hell do I know, right? I'm only eighteen. And *I'm a girl.*"

Dr. Slikowski nodded, eyes on the road now. For a moment he said nothing. Then he surprised her with a word.

"True."

Jenna gaped at him. "What?" she snapped, forgetting for a moment how she was supposed to behave around the boss. "Are you saying—"

"No," he said quickly, shaking his head. "Detective Flannery and the other officer behaved like perfect idiots. Flannery, at least, ought to know better. As a detective, it's dangerous business to assume anything about anyone on first sight.

"But I'm not surprised, and neither should you be. The way they responded to you is just human nature. Putting aside the gender issue, you are quite young. The only way we old folks can sleep at night is to tell ourselves how much brighter we are than the next generation. It helps us feel better about being old."

Jenna laughed a little at that.

"I'm serious," Dr. Slikowski told her. "You're going to get that, if you continue to work with me. And I hope you will. You have a keen mind, Jenna. In any case, I meant what I said. I thought you handled them well."

"But Flannery didn't believe me anyway," she argued. "And I'm not even sure if you do."

Slick smiled. "You know I don't like to make any statements regarding an autopsy before it's complete," he reminded her. "However, unless something unforeseen pops up in Dyson's notes, I think our friend Joe Flannery's going to be a bit surprised when he receives my report indicating our recommendation that they look at both men of small stature and women as potential suspects."

Jenna smiled the whole ride back to Somerset.

By the time they got back to SMC, it was quitting time for Jenna. Dyson was out of the office, so she just said good-bye to Dr. Slikowski and headed for home. The sun had disappeared behind clouds again, though there were still patches of blue. But even the blue sky was draining of color as evening approached. Jenna shivered as she walked across Carpenter Street, then started across the quad. She wished she'd brought her jacket after all.

Jenna was still happy that Dr. Slikowski had been so encouraging and supportive, but the buzz from it was starting to wear off. And as it did, she found her mind going back to the way the cops had treated her at the crime scene. The uniformed officer had been downright rude, but in some ways, that wasn't as bad as the way Detective Flannery had brushed off even the possibility that she might have something of value to contribute.

Instead of growing frustrated, or even sad, however, Jenna was starting to get very angry. She was aware of her anger, was withdrawn enough from it that she could analyze and understand it.

But that didn't make it go away.

So let's do something with it, she thought.

When she got upstairs to her room, Yoshiko wasn't around. *Probably off having dinner with Hunter,* Jenna thought. She knew she should eat something, but found that she wasn't very hungry.

There were no messages on her answering machine, so she sat down at the computer and went on-line. She had three e-mail messages. One was spam. One was from Dyson, teasing her about being the "teacher's pet." She knew she'd get some ribbing from him when she went in on Friday. The last message was from Moira Kearney, one of her best friends from high school. Moira was at USC, hoping to break into film-making. Her e-mail said she'd taken a role in a student film production, which made Jenna laugh to herself.

She typed back one word in reply: "Actors!"

Then she set about typing the one e-mail that felt important to her right now. This one was to the third girl who'd made up their trio of musketeers in high school, Priya Lahiri. Priya was at Northwestern, in Illinois, and she'd been a bit homesick. Jenna had been very supportive, and they'd e-mailed a lot and talked a few times, despite the long-distance bill.

But now she had something to keep Priya occupied.

Hey Pri,

Since I know you have nothing better to do, I

thought you might like to help me solve a murder! :)
Seriously. I don't know how much you know about Indian religion and stuff, and I know your folks aren't
the most orthodox Hindus. Okay, they're wacky. (Who
said that? Blake!) *LOL* Anyway, I saw some weird
pictures earlier. Paintings, actually. One of them is
supposed to be of Shiva, if that rings any bells. Four-
armed guy doin' the two-step on top of a corpse. Then
there was a moon with a skull face or death mask or
something on it. The last one was a guy with the head
of an elephant.

I know it's all just freak-mash, but see if you can
make anything out of it for me. I'll owe you, as usual.
Grape jelly beans, on me.

—Forgot one more. Somebody drew a circle or
something on the guy's forehead in black marker. The
dead guy, I mean, not one of the paintings.

If you come home to visit, you'd better call!

Love ya, kiss ya, already miss ya . . .
—Lady J

Jenna read the e-mail over quickly, then hit Send. She
nodded resolutely, pleased with herself, but it wasn't
enough. She spent ten minutes doing an on-line search,
but didn't come up with anything really helpful, mostly
just generalities. Frustrated, she shut down the computer and stared at the blank screen for several seconds.
It might be days before Priya responded to her e-mail.
Jenna had never been known for her patience.

Why wait, when I can hit the library? Beloved destination of students everywhere!

This time, she made sure she put on her leather jacket and zipped it up tight. Then she grabbed a notebook and some pens, stuffed them in her bag, and headed out.

There were small squares all over Somerset and Cambridge where businesses and restaurants thrived. People wanted to live there, and with the college crowds, there was always someone to spend money. But somehow, all that prosperity never seemed to reach Kettle Square. Restaurants closed and opened on an almost monthly basis. Merchants disappeared overnight, running out on their leases. About the only things that stayed for very long, for whatever reason, were beauty salons.

The Kettle Square Café had been shut down for a week. Inside, it had been stripped so bare it seemed as if the Grinch had been there. All the businesses around it were closed by eight o'clock, save for a Papa Gino's pizza place down the block.

Stephanie Tyll was running late. *Jimmy's gonna be pissed*, she thought as she hurried along the cracked sidewalk toward Papa Gino's. She didn't really know why she was worried about that. Sure, Jimmy got mad now and again, but he'd never hit her. He wouldn't either. She trusted him. Still, she didn't like to see him angry.

At twenty-three, Stephanie still lived at home. She

wanted to move out, but she just didn't have the money. Not with what she made as a receptionist at the weight-loss clinic on the other side of the square. But together, she figured she and Jimmy could swing it.

If only he'd ask. Then I could be free.

Stephanie froze in the middle of the sidewalk, and laughed at herself.

"That's a pretty stupid way to think," she said aloud.

After all, she reasoned, here she was worrying because she was a few minutes late meeting Jimmy at Papa Gino's, and she was thinking being with him would make her free.

All of a sudden Stephanie Tyll knew she had some thinking to do. Still, she wasn't about to keep Jimmy waiting. She started off for Papa Gino's again, walking past the Kettle Square Café's windows, which had been frosted over after it shut down.

She heard the click of the door opening as she passed.

Startled, Stephanie turned around to see a woman looking at her in a friendly way, like she was about to ask her something. Then she noticed the little black thing in the woman's hand, maybe the size of a cell phone.

Then the woman touched her with it, and tens of thousands of volts of electricity passed through her body. She stiffened, grunting in pain, and then she blacked out.

The woman caught Stephanie before she could fall

and dragged her into the darkness of the restaurant, behind the frosted glass.

It took Stephanie Tyll a long time to die. But she was lucky, in a way. The shock from the taser kept her unconscious. She never had to see what was being done to her.

c h a p t e r   4

The phone was ringing. Eyelids flickering, hovering between sleep and waking like a paper clip suspended between two magnets, Jenna dreamed/imagined that she had used her finger, cocked like a pistol, to shoot at the phone.

For some reason this handgun had no effect.

The phone was still ringing.

Jenna snapped awake on the third ring. She was already out from under her sheets and halfway across the room before she was even truly aware that she was awake. Though she found herself with an odd compulsion to shoot at the phone, she lifted it from its cradle.

"Hello?" she asked groggily as she glanced over at the clock on Yoshiko's desk.

7:01.

"It's seven in the morning," she told the caller.

It was her father.

"Jenna, I'm sorry to wake you, honey," he said quickly. "I'm just getting ready for the day, having breakfast, and I only just now got around to listening to my messages from yesterday."

Jenna blinked. She'd been so wrapped up in things yesterday afternoon, and so wrapped up in sleeping until a second ago, that she'd sort of put out of her mind that her dad had blown her off for lunch the day before.

Or I was just blocking it out?

"Yeah, where were you yesterday?" she demanded.

"I'm just way behind on the book. After my morning class, I sort of locked myself in, went incommunicado, turned off the ringer, everything. I worked straight through until about four hours ago, and I just woke up and remembered the messages and—"

"So you just totally forgot we had a lunch date?" she asked, not bothering to hide how hurt she was.

On the top bunk, she saw Yoshiko stir and sit up, rubbing her eyes and yawning.

"Not totally," her father said tentatively. "But I did forget it was yesterday. I'm sorry, Jenna. I'll make it up to you."

"I'll put it on your tab, Dad. You're still busy working off every other time in the last eighteen years you weren't there when you said you were going to be," Jenna said.

There was a moment of silence on the other end of the line. Jenna turned toward the sink so Yoshiko wouldn't see how upset she was becoming, but then she looked into the mirror, and could see her room-mate behind her. Yoshiko looked astonished.

"Jenna," her father said at length. "That's not fair."

"No? Well, take it up with the fairness committee," she replied, but her anger was weakening. "Look, Dad, I know you're busy. So am I. I'm a big girl. I just . . . oh, forget it. What about today?"

Frank sighed. "I'm afraid I can't today, Jenna. I'm having lunch with—"

"Shayna. Got it. Never mind."

"Not with Shayna. I'm meeting with the publisher in Boston. And I thought you liked Shayna."

"I do." Jenna sighed.

"Good. Let's all have dinner, the three of us, and any-one you'd like to bring. Tomorrow night. Anywhere you like," Frank suggested. "Can you make it?"

Jenna thought about it. But only for a second. "Pick me up in the lot behind Sparrow at six," she told him. "Also, I'm going home on Sunday to take Mom out for her birthday. It'd be nice if you came along."

"Let me see how much work I get done," her father said.

But she knew he'd never do it.

After they said their good-byes and hung up, Jenna looked up at Yoshiko and smiled wearily. "Morning."

"Morning," Yoshiko replied. "He didn't make it for lunch yesterday, huh?"

Jenna laughed. "You got that, huh? Listen, you and Hunter want to come with us to dinner tomorrow night? Dad's wallet will be suffering."

"That's not like you," Yoshiko said, frowning slightly.

"Call it payback," Jenna said.

There was a moment while Yoshiko considered it that Jenna was sure she'd say no. It confirmed everything she had feared about her belief that they were growing apart, that Yoshiko's relationship with Hunter was hurting their friendship.

Then Yoshiko smiled. "Sounds good. I'll have to check with Hunter, but you can count me in."

"Then I can count him in, too," Jenna said. "After all, if you're there, Hunter can't be far behind. By the way, have we progressed to using 'boyfriend' and 'girlfriend' yet?"

"You'll be the first to know," Yoshiko replied.

While Yoshiko was in the shower, Jenna checked her e-mail to see if there was any reply from Priya. She didn't really expect anything so quickly, but found herself disappointed when the only e-mail she had was a joke from her friend Noah Levine, who was at UMass Amherst. Then she read it. "Twenty-five Things a Woman Will Never Say to a Man," it was called. It was filthy. But it was also funny.

Jenna was still giggling when Yoshiko came back into the room. When Yoshiko read it, she blushed. But she laughed too.

By the time Jenna got back from showering, Yoshiko had already gone to class. She dressed quickly, dried her hair, and then grabbed her bag to head out to her American lit class. They'd spent the past few weeks discussing genres, and for today's class, they'd read a Mickey Spillane novel called *One Lonely Night*. Jenna had enjoyed the book, in spite of its outdated feel. There was something almost quaint about the Neanderthal heroics of Spillane's main character.

Men, she thought, as she pulled the door closed behind her and headed down the hall. After a moment, though, she turned around and walked in the other direction.

She stopped in front of Damon's door and knocked.

After a few seconds, someone mumbled something unintelligible from inside. Then she heard the lock sliding back, and the door opened to reveal the sleepy, unshaven face of Harry Gershman, Damon's roommate. The room was dark, heavy shades pulled down to block out the sun.

Harry looked a bit startled to see her. Which might have had something to do with the boxer shorts that were all he had on.

"Jenna!"

"Morning, Harry. Damon at class?"

"No. I'm here," came a deep voice like a growl from the top bunk in the darkness of the room.

Damon sat up, sheets covering him from the waist down. He smiled tiredly and scratched the back of his head.

"Hey," Jenna said. "Guess I'm not exactly catching you at your best."

He grinned, wrapped the sheet around his waist and slipped down from the bunk. "I'm always at my best," Damon said cockily.

Jenna knew it was only an act, and rolled her eyes. "Right. Listen, I just wanted to know if you were free for dinner later. Figured we could catch up, maybe hang out after. Rent a movie."

"You asking me on a date?" Damon inquired, eyes narrowing quizzically.

"Thought we tried that already," Jenna replied, smiling. "But if you're threatened, you can bring Harry along to protect you."

"Nah, that's cool." Damon laughed. "Sure. What, Nadel, like, five-thirty?"

"Sounds good." She looked at Harry. "You can pick the movie."

Harry blinked. "Me? Uh-uh. I don't want to be a third wheel. A little too funky for me, chaperoning a date."

"It's *not* a date," Jenna said firmly.

With a grin, Harry shrugged. "Sure. It's important you believe that. But y'know, Jenna, now you've seen Damon in the all together, it's gonna be hard for you to control—"

Damon pulled the pillow off his bunk and whacked Harry in the back of the head, cutting off the rest of his brilliant insight.

"Man, you will so regret that," Harry said, grinning even more broadly.

"See ya, guys," Jenna said, shaking her head. "If I wanted this, I'd be flipping channels in search of reruns of *American Gladiators*. Have fun."

Even as she stepped out, Damon shouted, "Goodbye," and tackled Harry, both of them crashing against the door. It slammed shut with a bang that Jenna figured woke up anybody else on the floor fortunate enough not to have classes first thing in the morning.

When she walked out of Sparrow Hall, Jenna was surprised at how nice the weather was. The day before had been so gray and depressing. But today was a completely different story.

Things were looking up.

After Jenna got out of Professor Georges's European history class that afternoon, she walked right past Sparrow Hall without even glancing at it. Most of the day, her mind had been returning again and again to the murder scene at the edge of the Charles River. That, and the attitudes of the two Cambridge cops she'd met. She was mature enough to realize that just because those two had acted like complete jerks didn't mean every cop in their department would behave the same way. But it was hard not to think of them as a group.

It was odd, in a way. Since Danny was her image of a Somerset cop, and that sexist idiot Flannery was what came to mind when she thought of Cambridge cops, she knew she was building up a prejudice that she couldn't afford if she meant to stay in this job.

For the moment, though, she was still ticked off enough to be determined to solve the murder before they did. Or, at the very least, give them a lead that would lead to a solution. Then they'd owe her.

There was something delicious about that.

So instead of going back to her room, Jenna kept right on walking, across Carpenter Street, and back to SMC. She didn't have to work that afternoon, but she knew that Dyson would be there, even if Slick was elsewhere.

Sure enough, when she knocked on the door, Dyson called out for her to come in.

"Hey," he said with surprise as he looked up from his computer.

"Hey yourself," she said.

"So how'd it go yesterday?"

"Could have been better," she grumbled.

"I heard you scored big points," he said. "You don't think so?"

"Maybe you also heard what morons the cops were to me," she said. When Dyson raised his eyebrows and smiled thinly, she knew Slick had told him all about it. "Good," she said. "Then you know I'm pissed. Color me motivated."

Dyson laughed. "All right, I'll play along. How can I help?"

"The ashes Dr. Slikowski found on Bill Broderick's body. He sent them up to the lab. I was hoping you could tell me the results," she said, sort of hedging.

"Y'know, Jenna, I'm sure that Slick will include you on this one. He wouldn't have brought you down there if he wasn't planning on it. Plus, you know he gets a kick out of just listening to your theories. Your mind works differently from his, and he likes having that perspective around," Dyson explained.

Jenna felt a bit awkward, and glanced away. "I guess

I knew that, but I never really thought of it like that," she said. "Still, though, I feel like it's personal now. Because of the way those guys acted."

Dyson shrugged. "The results came back this morning. The ashes are human."

With a sigh, Jenna shook her head. "Why did I have a feeling it was going to be something like that?" She glanced up and saw that Dyson had a big grin on his face. "What?" she demanded.

"That's just the way you think."

"So where did the ashes come from?" she asked.

"That's the million-dollar question, isn't it?" Dyson asked. "Certainly no way to identify them now. You have to figure the jogger didn't have them on his clothes naturally. Especially since there's a ritual murder element to this thing. But if we could figure out where he or she got the ashes, we might not need to figure out what the ritual was all about."

Jenna contemplated that for a second, then she just nodded. "Thanks, Dyson. I guess I'll see you tomorrow, okay?" She turned to leave.

"Hey," Dyson called.

She paused in the doorway.

"Don't you want to know what the cause of death was? I mean, according to the autopsy results?" he asked, smiling.

"Why?" Jenna asked. "Did you find something we weren't expecting?"

"No. But it wasn't official until today, and you know the rules."

"Yeah." She laughed. "Gotta know 'em to break 'em."

Her room was empty when she returned to Sparrow Hall. But there was a note from Yoshiko taped to the front of her computer.

Hey, Jenna.

Turns out we can't make dinner tomorrow night after all. Hunter had already made other plans for us. Maybe this weekend? Sorry.

—Yoshiko

Jenna felt something flip-flop in her stomach as she read the note. That morning, she had been feeling a lot better about her life and her friends. She'd realized that it wasn't so much that she needed to talk about Melody as she needed to move on with life in her absence. But now she was back to square one.

So it'll be just me, Dad, and Shayna. Yippeee, she thought. *I think I was in love with the idea of them being in love. But I liked her better when she wasn't the competition.*

With a sigh, she crumpled the note up and tossed it in her trash can. Then she booted up her computer and checked her e-mail. Still nothing from Priya. But that wasn't going to keep her from doing more research just the same. The previous night's trip to the library had been very informative.

Many of the symbols used in the murderer's ritual were from ancient Hinduism, the religion of India.

Even now, Jenna flipped over a book she'd taken out from the library and began to search for more information on the Internet. She spent three-quarters of an hour doing that, and didn't learn much more than she already knew from her previous research.

It seemed that most of the symbolism in the ritual revolved around the Hindu god Shiva. The image of the four-armed god dancing on a dead man was a common representation of Shiva. The god, according to Hindu myth, lived in the cremation grounds, and if he was cut, human ashes would flow from his veins.

But those ashes didn't flow from anybody's veins, Jenna thought. *So where did they come from?*

Shiva had three eyes, the third found in the center of his forehead, which explained the black circle the killer had drawn on Broderick's face. Jenna had also found references to the skull and moon as symbols of Shiva, but didn't quite understand their significance.

As for the elephant-headed man, she figured that was supposed to be Ganesha, who was the Hindu god of scribes and merchants. She had not a single clue as to what Ganesha had to do with the ritual. Whatever it was, it was some ancient bit of occult cruelty that she just couldn't begin to understand.

What she could do, however, was use the Internet to begin searching for connections to individuals. It might not be necessary for her to understand the purpose of the ritual at all. There was more involved in the murder than just Hindu religion. It had to do with Hindu magic and mysticism. Jenna didn't believe in those things, but obviously the killer did. So the key was for her to track down individuals in the Boston area who had knowledge of and faith in ancient Hindu mysticism.

As far as Jenna was concerned, Internet search engines were like blunt knives: they did the job, but in a very sloppy fashion. She spent two hours cross-referencing, checking this link and that, trying different word combinations. By accessing academic and religious sites, she managed to find a number of people in the vicinity who might be considered scholars in ancient Hindu traditions and faith. It was certainly a start. When she had a chance, she'd have to start getting more information on them individually, something she could also use the Internet for, since most of them seemed to have written something or other, or lectured somewhere.

But not tonight. It was already five o'clock, and she was due to meet Damon at Nadel at five-thirty.

Jenna stretched, checked her e-mail one more time to see if Priya had replied, and came up with nothing. She brushed her hair and changed her clothes. Dinner at the dining hall and a movie from Hillside Video wasn't a date, but that didn't mean she shouldn't look nice. Capri pants, a cotton jersey with a matching sweater, and blue Steve Madden flats, and she felt much better.

I'm a whole new me. No more grumpy Net-grrrl. Now sweet and sassy college chick.

She looked in the mirror and decided she looked sort of tired.

Or not. But at least I'm trying.

When she got to the DH, she found Damon waiting out in front with Caitlyn and Olivia. He always looked good, and that afternoon was no exception. He had on a brown knit shirt and khaki pants, with shoes that looked very expensive. Even though it was casual, it was the kind of outfit most of the guys she'd gone to high school with wouldn't be caught dead in, because it was just a bit too classy.

But Damon was obviously very comfortable. You had to have confidence to dress well. Of course, he often wore blue jeans and sneakers and sweatshirts.

And he looks just as good in those as he does now.

Not for the first time, Jenna thought that maybe the possibility of the two of them getting together wasn't as much of a dead end as she'd believed. On the other hand, she felt like she needed friends right now, and no way was she going to blow their friendship just because she found him attractive.

"Hey!" he said amiably as she walked up.

"You were early," she said, surprised. "That's new."

"Shattering my image on a daily basis. It's my new hobby," Damon declared.

"You guys eating with us?" Jenna asked the girls, after they'd exchanged greetings.

Caitlyn smiled warmly. "If you don't mind the company."

Before Jenna could remind them that she and Damon were just friends, and assure them that they should all sit together, Olivia gave Caitlyn an annoyed look and cut in.

"Actually, we'll pass," she said. "Cait and I have some stuff to discuss. Sorority stuff, y'know? I'm sure you guys would be majorly bored, and we don't want to cramp your style, anyway."

Anyone else, saying this last, would have smiled to show that they were teasing. Olivia wasn't smiling.

"Okay," Jenna said, shrugging. "Cool."

But it didn't feel cool. In fact, it felt bad. Wrong. And later, after she and Damon had gotten their food and sat down, she couldn't prevent herself from bringing it up.

"So Olivia has it bad for you, huh?" she asked him.

Damon frowned and then twisted his face up into a smile of disbelief. "You've got to be kidding. Uh-uh. I mean, we get along and all, but that girl puts herself so high on a pedestal she'd never deign to look down far enough to see me. In a romantic sense, I mean. It's fine to hang out and stuff, but I'm not her type at all."

He looked at her seriously then. "Why would you say that?" he asked.

"Just a feeling I had," Jenna told him. "I mean, we're sort of friends. Or, at least, we have been. Gotta say, I'm finding this whole college friendship thing to be more complicated than it looked at first glance. Anyway, she's just been weird to me lately, and it always seems to be around you.

"I mean, there's nothing real gender-specific going on between us—"

"That's a hell of a way to put it," Damon said. "I like that."

"Point is, I know it and you know it, but I keep thinking Olivia's getting pretty jealous because she doesn't know it."

Damon was chewing, and had to swallow before he could respond. Then he just shook his head and shrugged, like what he was saying was completely unimportant. Like it meant nothing at all. "It's not jealousy," he told Jenna. "It's a race thing."

She blinked. "I'm sorry?"

"Olivia thinks something's up with us, and it bugs her because you're white. She figures if I'm smart enough to go to Somerset and will probably end up with a decent job and all, then I should be with a black woman instead of a white one. Keep it all in the family, you see what I'm saying?"

Damon kept eating, as if that explanation were enough.

Jenna stared at him, barely able to comprehend what he'd said, so foreign was the concept to her. She had known that when they'd dated before, some of his friends had not wanted Damon to go out with her because she was white, but she had assumed that was just racism. Or at least prejudice against interracial relationships. But this was something completely different. This was a cultural attitude. Something she had no frame of reference from which she might even begin to understand.

"Is that, like, common? That attitude, I mean?" Jenna asked.

Damon had to think about that a moment. He nodded slowly. "It's not uncommon, if that's what you mean. It's not just Olivia, in other words."

"What do *you* think?" Jenna asked.

He grinned. "I think it's not a date, so it doesn't matter what I think. And, anyway, I think you know what I think."

Jenna chuckled. "You think?"

"I think."

They rented *The Maltese Falcon* that night. They couldn't decide on anything from the new release shelf, and Damon loved Bogart. Jenna had never seen it, and knew it was a classic, so she agreed. Turned out she found herself to be sort of a Bogart fan as well, though she thought the whole hard-boiled thing was a little silly.

On the other hand, she wasn't sure if she'd given it a fair shake. The conversation at dinner had set a certain tone for the night that kept Jenna from completely relaxing around Damon. The fact that he was not the same race as she was had never been an issue to her.

And now it was. But not for any reason she might ever have imagined.

When she kissed him on the cheek as he left to go back to his room—a friendly peck, like she always gave him—she found herself remembering what she'd told him earlier that night. *I'm finding this whole college friendship thing to be more complicated than it looked at first glance.*

That was turning out to be quite an understatement.

When she slipped into bed, Jenna found it difficult to

fall asleep. Her mind was spinning with so many thoughts, about the Broderick murder and those cops and her friends and her family and her classes—she'd blown off reading her history assignment and would have to do it in the morning—that it was quite some time before she finally drifted off.

Even then, her sleep was troubled.

Haunted by the image of a man with the head of an elephant.

In Kettle Square the police had finally taken Stephanie Tyll's parents seriously. They'd questioned her boyfriend for a while, and come up with nothing. She'd left home to meet him at Papa Gino's and apparently never shown up. Following her route was the most obvious course of action, the very first thing they did.

It wasn't long before they found that the door to the Kettle Square Café wasn't locked.

Sergeant Claire Bellamy was the first one into the restaurant. It was dark in there, but the power was still on, so she flicked the light switch, and found what was left of Stephanie Tyll.

Sergeant Bellamy had never thrown up in front of a fellow officer before. She found it mightily embarrassing.

c h a p t e r 5

Danny Mariano hated the night shift. Always had. But as homicide detective for the City of Somerset, he and his partner, Audrey Gaines, were required to do one overnight a week. When the call had come in tonight about the Tyll girl, hell, it'd almost seemed like destiny. Lately, it seemed like Mariano and Gaines caught all the nasty ones.

And just from what they'd already heard, Danny knew this was going to be nasty. He piloted their unmarked along the main roads of Somerset, gliding unhurriedly toward Kettle Square. They were in no rush to get to the scene.

Danny put voice to his thoughts. "I hate nights."

"Why?" Audrey asked.

He looked at her as though she were insane. "What do you mean, 'why'? Wouldn't you rather do a day shift?"

"It's an ugly job," Audrey said, then shrugged. "Guess it doesn't matter if it's day or night. In some ways, night's better. The kinds of things we see, you shouldn't have to see in the daylight."

Danny turned his attention back to the road and chewed on that one. It came to him after a moment, why he felt the way he did about the night. He almost didn't want to mention it, didn't want to have to put it into words, but he'd brought it up, after all.

"You're right," he told her. "I guess that's part of it. This kind of stuff should only happen at night. But going into the scene when it's dark out, I always feel like it isn't over yet. Like it could get worse, and that might include us.

"When we catch a case on a day shift, go to the scene, then it feels like it's over. We're the cleanup crew, and it's our job to make it right. But at night . . . I just don't like it."

There was silence in the car for a couple of minutes, as Danny drove into Kettle Square. Ahead, blue lights from several patrol cars spun silently, splashing color off the buildings of the square. They pulled up in front of the restaurant where the girl's body had been found, and Danny killed the engine.

"Nothing to worry about here," Audrey said as they got out. "By all accounts, this one is definitely over."

Danny said nothing, but part of him wanted to argue. This kind of crime, as ugly as it was, wouldn't ever be over. Not even if they caught the killer and put him away. Not as long as there were people who cared about the girl and remembered the savage things that had been done to her.

Prepared for the worst, Danny followed Audrey into the restaurant, nodding to Sergeant Bellamy as he stepped through the door. But what he found inside was so much worse than he could have imagined.

The girl's been hacked to pieces.

Danny tried to think of another word for it, but couldn't. As he entered the restaurant, he saw the blood spattered all over the floor and one wall. There was a line of blood spray dried on the inside of the frosted-over windows as well. But blood wasn't all that had flown when the killer set to work. There were pieces of the girl strewn about the floor as well.

Jagged ribs protruded from her open chest cavity. Stained white bone was laid bare on her arms and legs, even her skull gleamed in the harsh, surreal light of the empty restaurant.

As he looked at it, two thoughts filled Danny's mind. He could not escape them, not even long enough to concentrate on his work. The first was his astonishment that any human being could be so relentlessly savage—what had been done in that place had taken a long time. He didn't know it was possible to sustain rage that long. And there was no doubt in his mind that whoever had done this had been enraged. It wasn't done for fun, and it wasn't done for passion, and it wasn't done out of clinical sociopathic curiosity.

It was done out of rage.

The second thought that Danny could not banish

from his mind was this: *Oh God, her parents.* The idea that the girl's parents would have to see her like this, even on that cold slab in the morgue to identify her . . . the idea that they would even have to know how she died.

A part of Danny Mariano froze over inside as he stood in the empty space that had once been the Kettle Square Café. That was the only way he could continue to do his job that night. Maybe he'd thaw when the sun came up, and maybe not. He didn't really know.

When he finally looked over at Audrey, he could see from the hard glint in her eyes and the set of her jaw that she was frozen as well. Then it hit him. For the first time, he realized a fundamental truth about Audrey, a woman he'd been partnered with for years. She'd been a homicide cop a lot longer than he had. Danny had witnessed real horror in his job, but Audrey must have seen so much more.

Maybe part of her froze up and never thawed.

The thought made him intensely sad for her.

Then there was the girl. He forced himself to walk closer, to move past her, to examine what was left of her body and the area around where she'd been killed. As he moved deeper into the room, he saw the scrawl for the first time. The pictures had been spray-painted in white on the linoleum. The body partially obscured one of them.

"Jesus," he whispered.

Even as he turned to Audrey, she moved up beside him. "Like the one in Cambridge," she said, her voice a bit throatier than usual. "But I read the report on that. There was nothing like this. It was a straight strangulation. There wasn't this . . . mess."

"Something set him off," Danny said, suddenly certain of it. "All this ritual crap, it's supposed to do something. Whatever it is isn't happening, and he's angry."

The ice inside him spread a little farther as he turned to Audrey again. "And if he's not getting what he wants, that means he's going to keep trying."

Friday morning the sky was gray, and it promised to remain that way for the balance of the day. Jenna didn't mind. It reflected her mood. She realized that she'd been on a kind of emotional rollercoaster recently, up one minute and down the next. Manic depression, maybe, but she didn't think it was really all that bad. In the wake of Melody's murder, she was trying to find a new center for her life. That center had been Jenna *and* Melody, the way things happen with the most intimate of friends.

But the center's gotta be just me.

Even though her mood was gray, that realization had seemed to crystallize things for her. She was happy for Hunter and Yoshiko, and if their being together meant they weren't there for her as much, she would deal. Same with her father, and his new relationship with Shayna, though she was looking forward to her dinner with them that night.

And Damon . . . that was a completely different story. He was a friend. She had no idea if she wanted more out of it, but until she decided for sure, she wasn't about to start some kind of sniping match with Olivia Adams over the politics of interracial dating.

Jenna pushed it all behind her, determined to go only forward.

The two things she held on to were the way the Cambridge cops had treated her, and her vow to keep going after the murderer. She hadn't heard from Priya yet, but she planned to call her that night if there was still no e-mail response. And she'd do some more research as soon as she could.

And she'd talk to Slick. He had confidence in her, had taken her under his wing. So much of what had been good in her life in the past weeks had come from working for him, and from his faith in her, that she wanted to talk to him about the avenue of inquiry she'd been following. The one thing she didn't want was for him to dismiss it as some sort of crusade because the cops had been such jerks to her.

Which it is, Blake. Don't forget that.

Which it was. But that didn't make it less worth doing. Just that morning, she'd been sitting at her desk, checking her e-mail and fiddling with a new brainteaser puzzle that began in the shape of a simple box but could be manipulated into a double helix if one worked at it long enough. Jenna had always had both a love and a knack for such things, and that's what Slick's cases were: brainteasers. Only with those puzzles, the answers mattered to a lot of people.

Sometimes, the answers to them could save lives.

So she'd trump the cops and she'd talk to Slick and she'd move forward. Only forward. Jenna was determined.

She was super alert in her classes that day, and when she was done, she went straight to work, eager to see Dr. Slikowski. But when she reached the office, the door was locked. She let herself in, and found a note from Dyson on her desk.

J,

Got a real nasty one. Dr. S. wants you to come down. I think you should stay put. You'll thank me later.

Dyson

If she'd been in a different frame of mind, she might have paid attention to Dyson's warning. If Dr. Slikowski really needed her there, Dyson would never have advised her to stay in the office and do paperwork and transcription. But Slick wanted her at the scene. Which meant he wanted her *in on it*, whatever it was.

It gave her a thrill to know that. And she didn't want that feeling, or his inclination to include her, to ever go away. Dr. Slikowski had made her part of the team, and Jenna wasn't about to turn her back on that.

She locked the door behind her and headed down to the basement. When she got off the elevator and started down the corridor, she spotted Danny and Audrey immediately. They were leaning against the outer wall of the autopsy room, sipping coffee and talking quietly. Audrey was all in black, except for the tan shirt under her jacket. Danny had on crisp new blue jeans and black sneakers, and a dark-red cotton V-necked sweater. He looked good.

Good enough to make Jenna's heart skip a beat.

For the most part, she'd tried to put thoughts of Danny Mariano out of her mind. She had a crush on him. She had to accept that, but that didn't mean she had to let it ruin her day. He was thirty-one, she was eighteen—almost nineteen!—and even though she knew he liked her too, it was obvious he didn't think a relationship was appropriate.

Audrey didn't think it was appropriate either. She'd never said anything to Jenna. Not exactly. But it was impossible to miss the disapproval on her face anytime Jenna flirted with Danny.

Still, he looked *good*.

Until she got up close enough to see how pale he was and the circles under his eyes, and how haunted he seemed. Audrey didn't look much better.

"You guys been up all night?" Jenna asked, teasing.

Both detectives shot her a look that told her instantly that she wasn't funny.

"Actually, yeah," Danny said.

"Sorry," she said sheepishly.

Danny shook his head. "Don't worry about it," he said. "Just a very long, really ugly night."

"Detective Mariano hates the night shift," Audrey said dryly.

"I'm guessing that's your DOA in there, then?" Jenna asked.

"Yeah," Danny said. "And trust me, if you don't have to go in there, don't. As far as I'm concerned, I don't ever want to go in that room again. If it wasn't part of the job—"

"There's the catch," Jenna said with a shrug. "Part of my job."

But even as she reached for the doorknob to enter the autopsy room, she began to feel a little queasy. If what was inside had Danny and Audrey that spooked . . . *maybe I should do some transcriptions after all.*

That was just her subconscious mind talking, though. Even as the thoughts came to her, she was already entering the room. Then it was too late for her to change her mind. She wasn't going to be able to unsee the savaged girl on the autopsy table.

"I told you it was bad," Dyson said, looking at her over the top of his mask as he sliced into the girl's lung on a stainless steel scale.

"You were right," Jenna said weakly.

Dr. Slikowski was watching her, so Jenna tried not to react as much as she would have liked to. He sat in his wheelchair, his mask pulled down off his face, and regarded her curiously. After a short pause, he cleared his throat.

"You don't have to be here, you know," he said. "We can talk about it later, go over the aspects of the case together if you like."

Jenna considered leaving. Then she changed her mind. Oddly enough, she realized that she wasn't staying to impress Slick, or even herself. She was staying because she was part of the team and it was her job, just like she'd told Danny. And it was an important one.

"I'll stay," she said. "I've seen worse in this room."

Which was true, but only partially. For while she had seen bodies with much more damage—from a fire or a car accident—she had never seen a human being so horribly mutilated by another human being. For a second, she thought she might cry.

I'll be damned if I'll cry in here, she told herself.

And that was that.

The autopsy continued. Jenna washed up and put on a gown, cap, and mask, and she helped Dyson not only weigh and select lab samples from the organs, but separate organs that had been so badly damaged they weren't immediately identifiable.

It took more than an hour, even though she'd arrived halfway through the process, for Slick to dictate his notes on the condition of the body, on all the slashes and cuts and stab wounds. It wasn't until Jenna backed off to give them room—her own part in it finished—that she noticed the marks on the girl's neck.

"Dr. Slikowski?" she said tentatively. "I guess I came in too late for this?"

He looked up at her, noticed that she was indicating the ligature marks on the DOA's neck, and blinked in surprise.

"I'm sorry, Jenna," he said. "I thought Dyson would have mentioned it in his note, or that the detectives might have said something. I suppose I wasn't really thinking about it at all. But you're right."

She recoiled slightly. "So, you're saying the cause of death—"

"Was strangulation, yes."

"And the rest of this was what, then?" she asked, almost frantic, trying unsuccessfully to keep from reacting to the horror she felt. "Exercise? This is someone's idea of fun?"

Slick said nothing, only looked at her grimly. Sadly. It was Dyson who spoke up.

"Gaines and Mariano have a theory," he told her. "They think the Hindu symbols really do signify some kind of ritual. Whatever it is, the killer is expecting it to work. When it doesn't, he . . ."

Jenna shook her head, taking it all in. Then she looked up at Dyson. "You said 'he.'"

Slick raised his eyebrows. "The detectives think the crimes are too savage for a woman to have committed. While it sounds sexist on the surface, it's true that most crimes of this nature are committed by men."

"Most," Jenna said. "Not all."

"We have to keep an open mind, Jenna," Slick chided her.

"Tell them that," she snapped.

Then she turned, unable to look at the body anymore, and stripped off her bloody gloves and tossed them in the hazardous-waste bin. After she'd taken the rest of her gear off, she glanced back at Slick.

"If it's okay with you, I'm going to head up. I'll transcribe something while I wait. Then . . . I'd really like to talk to you some more about this," she said tentatively.

"I had a feeling you would," he said. "And that's fine. See you shortly."

She left.

Danny and Audrey were still in the hallway.

"Anything?" Danny asked when she came out.

"A lot of things," she said. "You can talk to Dr. Slikowski about it, though. I mean, what do I know?"

With that, she started down the corridor. Danny came after her.

"Hey," he said.

Jenna stopped to look at him.

"Dyson told us about the way the Cambridge cops blew you off. That was stupid of them. But we're not the enemy, remember?"

She nodded, took a deep breath, and then even smiled a little. "Sorry," she said. "I didn't know until just a minute ago that it was the same killer. I'm pretty shaken, I guess. I have to tell you, though, you guys are wrong to just cross every female psycho off your list. I mean, there's logic and then there's logic, y'know?"

Danny thought about that for a second. "We're not going to completely dismiss the idea," he told her. "That would be dumb. But this isn't a completely dead space like the Charles was when the Broderick guy was killed. Kettle Square isn't necessarily alive and kicking, but there are people down there. If the killer was a woman, and according to our height estimates not exactly an Amazon, how did she drag the Tyll girl off the street without a struggle or a scream or anything?"

Jenna didn't have an answer for that. "Maybe she knew her?" she suggested, then shook her head. "Maybe she hypnotized her for all we know. I'm just saying don't count the possibility out. And maybe I'm just saying that because of the attitude I got from that jerk Flannery and his buddy."

She paused and took another breath. Then she looked up at Danny and managed a thin smile. "I want to get a Coke," she said. "Can I buy you another coffee? They'll be up in a minute."

Danny paused, then glanced down the hall at Audrey. "Just a second," he said, holding up a finger. He walked down and spoke to his partner for a few seconds, and then he came back to Jenna.

"Let's go," he said.

Before Jenna turned to walk with him to the elevator, she glanced at Audrey. The detective had one eyebrow raised. She smiled at Jenna, but it was a false smile, a what-the-hell-are-you-doing smile. Jenna knew it was meant for Danny more than it was for her, but she wanted to say "Don't jump to conclusions."

But she wondered if there were conclusions to jump to.

Coffee with Danny was harmless, but it was also nice. They talked about things other than the dead girl in the basement, and Jenna found herself opening up to him. More than that, she found him responding, opening up to her in return. Talking about his life to her for the first time.

"It's hard, sometimes, to find time for real life," he said as they sat across from each other in the office, she in her chair and he in Dyson's. "People who aren't on the job don't understand what I do, they don't understand the kind of mind set you have to get into to do it. To them, it's all cops and robbers, like something on television. They think they know me because they've seen *Law and Order.*"

"Must be hell on your love life," Jenna offered.

Danny smiled wanly. "I dated this girl, Kim, for a while, earlier in the year. She didn't understand why I had to change shifts all the time. There's no nine-to-five with this job. Not really. Anyway, you don't want to hear about all this."

Actually, I do, she thought.

"It's all right," she said. "I can sympathize. Most of my friends think this job is extremely weird. And I've had a few guys be very turned off by it. I think it's also 'cause their view of it is defined by what they've seen on TV and stuff. Nobody thinks about how important the answers are that the M.E. provides."

"Especially Slick," Danny agreed. "The guy's all over the place. He's always catching things other people don't. Hell, in all that gore, a lot of people might have missed that the girl down there was strangled."

Jenna shivered. "Yeah, but with the symbols, there's no question it had to be the same person."

Part of her wanted to talk to him about it, then to

tell him about her research. But now wasn't the time. All she had were bits and pieces of information, no explanations. Until she knew what the killer was trying to do, her research wasn't going to lead anywhere.

Or is it? Maybe it isn't knowing what the killer wants to do, but figuring out who could answer that question in the first place.

Then, as soon as the thought had come to her, she pushed it away. Now wasn't the time. She really didn't want to talk to Danny about it, not when it would just come out as so much brain mush. Facts first. Then she'd share.

Slick was another story. He'd see the way she was trying to put the pieces together. He'd understand.

She hoped.

"I'm surprised guys on campus wouldn't be more open-minded," Danny said dubiously. "I mean, this is an institute of higher learning, right?"

Jenna scowled. "You've got to be kidding."

Danny smiled. "Yeah. I am."

For a moment Jenna just stared at him, eye-to-eye with the one guy she really liked. He was so smart and funny, with plenty of that manly *Grrrr* to go around. And he was so unattainable.

And suddenly she didn't care.

"Do you think we could have dinner sometime?" she asked.

Danny blinked, eyes wide. He smiled uncertainly, blushing a bit. He opened his mouth, fumbling for something to say. Jenna held her breath, waiting for the embarrassment she fully expected to sweep over her.

Then the door swung open and Dyson stepped in, followed by Slick in his wheelchair, and Audrey bringing up the rear. The older cop looked at them, a little too closely, and Jenna saw that Danny was a bit flushed.

"So what's the verdict?" Jenna asked, mainly to distract them all from the possible awkward moment that was brewing.

"Our killer just doesn't care what we find," Dr. Slikowski declared grimly, wheeling himself in. "The savagery was not an attempt to hide the strangulation. But finding the strangulation, and amidst that savagery, we did almost miss a vital clue."

"Anyone else *would* have missed it," Dyson added, looking at Slick with open admiration.

"On the girl's skin we found twin burn marks. Electrocution. It wasn't the cause of death, but it's the key to this particular murder," the M.E. said.

Jenna was confused. "How's that?"

But Danny had already caught on. He was looking at Audrey, eyes narrowed.

"Taser?" he asked.

Audrey nodded.

"So now we know how the killer got Stephanie Tyll off the street without any noise or a struggle," Danny said. "Which leaves open the possibility that you're right. Psych profiles would say that the killings are too vicious to be a woman.

"But it's still *very* possible."

90

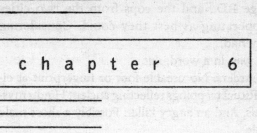

chapter 6

As the two detectives and the medical examiner's team discussed the murders, Jenna found herself being distracted by her growing embarrassment. Her conversation with Danny was what she had been waiting for, and now that it had come, she was unable to focus. At one point, Danny glanced at her, and Jenna looked away, feeling her cheeks flush red.

Oh, just stop, she chided herself. *You don't blush.*

But she did.

Despite all the reasons she knew she shouldn't have done it, Jenna had asked Danny on a date. They had a nice thing going, a nice rapport, and she figured she'd just thrown the whole thing into the garbage.

Good going, Blake.

With a sigh, she tried to focus on the conversation at hand. Thus far, it had been pretty much a rehash of things she already knew. Danny and Audrey were in communication with Joe Flannery at the Cambridge P.D., and the cops from the two cities were cooperating as best they could. Considering what they had.

Which was, in a word, *shit*.

Two murders. No useable foot or fingerprint at either site. Ritual trappings reflecting ancient Hindu mystical beliefs. And an angry killer. Possibly a short male or a female.

"What we need to do now is figure out the significance of the ritual elements here," Audrey Gaines said. "We're looking into the Hindu magick thing, but so far, it doesn't seem to resemble anything you'd find in modern Hindu worship."

Jenna glanced away. She hadn't really wanted to talk about this in a group. It would be better if she could just discuss it with Slick. But this did seem to be the opening.

"I've sort of been looking into that, too," she admitted.

Slick raised his eyebrows at her. The others turned to her as well. Danny smiled a little, but Audrey appeared very dubious, and Jenna understood why. They were the police. She was a pathology assistant. Her job had nothing to do with figuring out who the murderer was, just how the deed had been committed.

"Any progress?" Dyson asked thoughtfully.

Jenna shrugged. "Still working on it. I mean, we all know the whole Shiva thing. The eye on the forehead, the skull and the moon, they're all symbols of Shiva.

And the elephant man there is probably a Hindu god called—"

"Ganesha," Audrey interrupted.

Jenna blinked. "Yeah."

"As I said, we're looking into it. The question isn't what the symbols are, but what the overall purpose of the ritual is. Until we know that, or the perp kills again and leaves something useable behind, we're in the dark."

Danny frowned slightly at his partner, and Jenna hoped it was on her behalf. It was silly, in a way, but that didn't make the feeling go away. Audrey was being kind of a bitch, and Jenna didn't feel like she deserved it. Maybe she was too young for Danny, and maybe it was foolish of the two of them to be attracted to each other, but that didn't make any of it Audrey's business.

Jenna had a few other thoughts about how they might go about tracking down the killer, but suddenly she didn't feel like sharing them with Audrey Gaines.

"If anything occurs to you, let us know," Danny suggested.

"I'll do that," Jenna said dryly, shooting Audrey a hard look.

"I presume you've followed up on the human ash discovered on the bodies," Slick put in.

That gave them all pause. Jenna hadn't even thought to ask if there had been ash on the second body.

"We're working on it," Audrey replied.

Danny frowned more deeply. "Actually, Dr.

Slikowski, that was one of the questions we had for you. Is there any way someone could be getting cremated remains from a local hospital?"

Slick pondered that a moment. Then he sat up a little straighter in his wheelchair, and looked around at them. "Not really," he said. "If a limb or what have you is amputated, it might be cremated, but it would be disposed of with other hospital waste."

"And John Does aren't cremated," Dyson added. "We contact a local funeral home director and ask them to provide a state-funded welfare burial."

"So the only way to get ashes is if you've claimed those of a relative?" Audrey asked. "I mean, there were a lot of ashes at both murder sites."

Jenna almost bit her tongue as something occurred to her. Then she realized that keeping her mouth shut was sort of like letting Audrey push her around.

"What about funeral homes or mortuaries, wherever they do cremations?" she asked. "I mean, what do they do if someone has a family member cremated but never picks the ashes up?"

Everyone looked at her.

"We've looked into that," Audrey replied. "There haven't been any reports of breaking and entering or theft of ashes like that from any funeral home in the state in the past several years, which was what we could access using computer records."

Her face emotionless, Jenna looked at Audrey. "Do you honestly think if your business was the respectful disposal of people's remains, you'd want your customers to know you'd had some of those remains stolen out from under you?" she asked.

"An excellent point," Slick said proudly.

Danny grinned. "Yeah, guess we'd better look into that some more." He had been leaning against Jenna's desk, but he stood up as he said this, and moved toward the door. "Come on, Audrey. Back to the old drawing board."

Then he glanced at Jenna and smiled warmly. "I'll talk to you later," he said.

Audrey shook her head in disapproval, and Danny ignored her. Jenna decided to do the same.

When they'd left, Dyson looked over at Jenna. "I wasn't imagining that tension, was I?" he asked.

But it was Slick who responded. "No," he said. "You weren't. I don't understand it, either. Detective Gaines knows your father, Jenna. And up until now, she has always seemed to give you the respect we all feel you're due. Do you have any idea why she was so short with you?"

"I think I can guess," Dyson said, raising one eyebrow as he looked at Jenna.

But she didn't rise to his bait. She also wasn't about to have this conversation with Dr. Slikowski, of all people. So she lied.

"I honestly have no idea."

"It's so peculiar," Slick said.

But then his expression changed, and Jenna knew that the awkward moments had already passed from his head. He had more important things to worry about, like who was out there killing people.

"I'm going to take off, if that's all right with you, Walter," Dyson announced, glancing at his watch.

"Yes, fine. I suppose it's in the hands of the police now. Though I hate to have been asked for input and then not provided any real assistance," Slick replied. "Of course, don't think that means I'm giving up."

"Of course," Dyson repeated.

"You have a hot date or something?" Jenna asked him.

Dyson smiled and nodded. "Or something."

"*Well,*" Jenna said approvingly. "What's her name?"

Slick cleared his throat suddenly, and Jenna glanced over at him to see that he was looking at Dyson over the tops of his wire-rimmed glasses. Then she glanced back at Dyson, who was still smiling.

He lifted his chin slightly. "*Her* name is Doug."

Jenna's eyes widened slightly. All she said was "Oh." And then, as an afterthought, as a chuckling Dyson went out the door, she called after him. "Have fun!"

Then he was gone, leaving her alone with Slick, who didn't seem to be comfortable with what Jenna had just learned. For her part, Jenna had taken it in and moved on. She was more concerned with what she would say to Danny Mariano the next time they were alone together, and whether or not she could be of any help to them, since both the cops and Slick seemed to have things under control.

Or, as under control as they could be, considering the dearth of information so far in the case.

It was Slick who broke the momentary silence.

"So," the M.E. said, "what have you determined?"

"Huh?" she asked.

"In your research. You've been looking into this, I assume? Have you come up with anything the police haven't?"

"Not really," she confessed. "Although I'd have to say I'm working on a kind of profile of my own."

Slick nodded thoughtfully, gravely. "And what does your profile say about the killer?"

"Female. Eighteen to forty, give or take. Five three to five six. Intelligent. Maybe not from here originally, but certainly lives here now. Probably a scholar."

Silence followed her words, and Jenna grew uncomfortable. Slick seemed to be studying her with great interest. At length, he smiled, and crossed his hands on his lap.

"You keep to the female suspect in your profile mainly because it satisfies the need for something that would draw Bill Broderick underneath the bridge on the Charles," he began. "You guess eighteen to forty primarily because you feel any younger or older, and she would not be likely to have the strength to have strangled Broderick. Of course, I'd take issue with the upper end of the age parameters, but your point is taken.

"You judge her height based on Broderick's own, and the angle of the ligature marks we found on his neck. Her intelligence, if it is a female, is suggested by the precision with which she has gone about this ritual. Her knowledge of the Charles River and Kettle Square areas would seem to indicate a familiarity with the neighborhood," he conceded. "But what makes you think she's a scholar?"

Jenna glanced away, raised her eyebrows in a kind of minishrug. "I thought about the possibility that she might just have read this stuff somewhere and tried it out. But I didn't think that made much sense. We can't find the ritual, which means it's not common knowledge. I just don't think it's a cake recipe. It feels like something you'd need to understand—even if you were a psychopath—to attempt it."

She noticed the dubious expression on Slick's face.

"Not very scientific, is it?" Jenna asked.

"Not very, no," he replied. "But that doesn't mean it isn't true."

"Do you think it is?" She was suddenly hopeful. She knew it was a stretch, but it just seemed to make sense to her.

"I wouldn't rule it out," the M.E. replied politely. "Now perhaps we ought to wait until we have other information, and concentrate on the job at hand? Or, in your case, on dinner. It is time for you to go, isn't it?"

Jenna glanced at the clock on the wall. 5:30.

"Thanks for listening," she said, with a half smile, as she stood up and prepared to head back to her dorm.

"Not at all," Slick replied. "You know how much I value your input."

With that, he wished her good night and wheeled himself into his office. A moment later a raucous drum solo thundered through the air, and Slick was lost in his jazz again.

As she walked back to Sparrow Hall, Jenna couldn't help but be disappointed in the way things had gone. She knew, also, that it was more her fault than anything. Her anger at the way the police had treated her had not only driven her to look into these murders, but convinced her that somehow she had a lead nobody else would have. But when she tried to shine some light on what she believed she had to offer, she'd realized that there was almost nothing there. Just a few vague ideas and suspicions, none of which were really any help to anyone.

Then, of course, there was Danny. She still felt embarrassed at having asked him out. But also excited, even though she knew it would lead nowhere. It was sort of a thrill to have been so daring, even for only a few seconds.

When she turned her key in the lock and pushed open the door to Room 311, Jenna had a smile on her face. Then she saw Yoshiko and Hunter, standing in the middle of the room, arms around one another, breaking off from what had apparently been a passionate kiss. The smile disappeared from her face, to be replaced by a scowl of embarrassment.

"Sorry," she mumbled, and looked around awkwardly for an exit.

Yoshiko laughed nervously, moving away from Hunter, who shuffled a bit himself.

"God, don't be sorry," Yoshiko said. "It's your room, Jenna."

Jenna didn't smile. Her heart just wasn't in it. "It's our room," she said, and went past them with only the most cursory glance at each of them. She sat on her bunk and took off her shoes. Then she reached for the zipper on her pants, and stood up.

She looked at Hunter. "Hunt, I'm sorry, but I have to get ready for dinner with my father. Would you mind stepping out for just a minute?"

Hunter seemed confused at first, and Jenna knew that it was more her tone than her words that had thrown him. She glanced at Yoshiko, who also appeared taken aback.

"Sure, Jenna," Hunter replied after a moment's pause. Then he turned to Yoshiko. "I'll be right back."

Jenna was silent as he left the room. Then she quickly removed the clothes she'd been wearing that day. She went to the sink and washed her face, then applied some mascara and lipstick. In the mirror, she could see Yoshiko watching her, but Jenna didn't really feel like dealing with whatever remained unsaid between them. When she was through with the sink, she went to her closet and pulled out some khakis and a royal blue shirt and sweater combination that were very casual, but still looked great on her.

As she dressed, Yoshiko sat down at her desk, still watching Jenna in silence. Finally, it was Yoshiko who spoke up.

"What's going on with you?"

Jenna tucked in her shirt and glanced at Yoshiko with what she knew was a scowl. She regretted it, but could not stop the expression from spreading across her face.

"What are you talking about?" Jenna demanded.

"That," Yoshiko said, growing annoyed. She stood and gestured to Jenna. "That whole attitude. You've been so weird lately."

Jenna stared at her a moment, trying to decide whether she should speak her mind or not, whether it was worth the heartache of having that discussion at the moment. But she was too angry to allow herself any real say in the matter. Her mouth started working before she had even decided what to say.

"I haven't been weird," she snapped. "And if I had, how would you know?"

"What's that mean?" Yoshiko asked.

"It means that I know you guys are a thing now. Great. Happy for you. Fireworks and all. But try to understand just a little where that leaves me, will you? You and Hunter are the closest friends I've got. Melody's dead. You guys are too busy with each other to hang with me. I'm just feeling a lot of distance right now, and it kinda sucks. But you guys need to do your thing, and I'll have to deal.

"Is that what you wanted to hear?" Jenna asked, then turned away quickly, feeling incredibly stupid and needy for having told Yoshiko any of it.

She pulled the sweater on over the shirt and buttoned the two small buttons at the bottom. When she turned around to face her roommate again, she saw that all the anger had drained out of Yoshiko, who was now looking at her with a kind of wide-eyed sadness that Jenna had never seen in her before.

"That's not how it is, J," she said softly. "You know we love you. But I've gotta say, Hunter and I both thought you were keeping us at a distance."

"Como om!" Jenna said. "I invited you guys to dinner with my dad tonight. It was your choice to blow it off."

"It wasn't like that, Jenna," Yoshiko said quickly. "I explained it to you."

"Yeah, great."

There was a light knock on the door. Jenna ignored it, and slipped on her shoes as Yoshiko went to let Hunter in. When Jenna turned around and saw the expression on his face, she knew instantly that he'd been able to hear the conversation from outside the door.

"Eavesdropping?" she asked, feeling mean and petty even as she spoke.

Hunter didn't answer. Instead, he walked over to Jenna and put his arms around her. She fought it at first, but as he tried to pull her closer, she let herself go.

"She was my sister," Hunter whispered to her. "But I know you miss her, too. I understand. I'm sorry if we weren't paying you enough attention."

Jenna began to cry. It only lasted for a moment, and she felt silly as she stepped back a bit and wiped her hands across her eyes.

"Nah," she said. "Just me being selfish. I'm sorry, guys. I know you're just trying this whole boyfriend-girlfriend thing on for size, but I just . . ." She looked from Yoshiko to Hunter. "How do you do it?" she asked, looking at him as though for the first time. "How do you stand it?"

He was gravely serious as he gazed back at her. Then he pulled her close again.

"I can't stand it," he whispered. "But I'm not going to let it destroy my life. Melody would've kicked my ass good for that. Anytime you want to talk about her, or anything, you just come see me, all right?"

His voice had slid back into the southern twang of his roots, and Jenna found it oddly comforting.

"You too," she said.

Then she went to Yoshiko, who still seemed to be sad and uncomfortable. Jenna gave her roommate a powerful hug, and whispered an apology. Yoshiko returned the hug.

"All right," Yoshiko said after a moment. "You're late, and this is getting repulsive."

They all laughed at that. Together.

Halfway through their meal at the Dixie Kitchen in Boston, Frank Logan looked in wonder at his daughter, and grinned with pride and pleasure. All through the meal—a spicy Cajun feast that Frank knew he'd regret later—he'd been getting ganged up on by Jenna and Shayna, an old friend who had suddenly, and seemingly inexplicably, become his girlfriend. He still wasn't sure how it happened, but he was deliriously happy that it had.

Frank had been through two wives, and wasn't anxious to wed a third time. But there had been a kind of melancholy in his life for some time, and being with Shayna assuaged that considerably. Even gave him hope that one day, that melancholy would disappear for good.

At the moment, the two women were laughing and teasing him about the grease spot he'd just gotten on his new shirt.

"You can dress him up—" Jenna began.

"But you can't take him anywhere!" they finished together.

Frank just rolled his eyes and dabbed sheepishly at the stain. It wasn't ever going to come out. At least, not without whatever magic some people used for such things, a kind of sorcery he'd never been able to learn. But it didn't matter. Not at all. Jenna had grieved deeply after the death of her friend, and Frank knew he hadn't been much help, what with beginning his relationship with Shayna, and having to work night and day to finish his book, which was already past deadline.

He didn't know what had happened to lift her spirits, but he was delighted to see her smiling, to see her happy, and most importantly, to see her getting along so well with the woman with whom he was falling in love.

Jenna caught him looking at her, and shot him a suspicious glance.

"What's that look?" she demanded.

"Look?"

"That look," she insisted. "What is it?"

Frank smiled. "I just like that sound," he said.

"What sound?" she asked dubiously.

"The sound of my daughter laughing."

When Jenna got in that night, Yoshiko and Hunter were nowhere to be found, but that was all right. She felt better than she had since before Melody's murder. Her pique at the Cambridge cops, her embarrassment over being so bold with Danny, even her feeling that she'd been proving all of Slick's faith in her wrong . . . none of that meant anything in comparison to tonight.

She felt like she had her life back. Yoshiko and Hunter were there for her. The distance they'd created was gone. The same with her father. Jenna really did love Shayna, and always had. Tonight only cemented her feelings about how wonderful her father's new girlfriend was. His book was almost done.

All of sudden, it seemed, just in the course of a few hours, Jenna didn't feel alone anymore.

Energized, and feeling as though she wanted to share this good feeling with friends she hadn't heard from in a while, Jenna booted up her computer and prepared to write some e-mails, to reach out to people who meant something to her.

She had a single e-mail waiting.

It was from Priya.

chapter 7

Hey, Jenna!

Sorry it took me so long to get back to you. You know my parents aren't exactly traditional Hindu. :) Anyway, sounds like you've gotten yourself into yet another bizarro situation over there. I don't get you, Blake. The rest of us spend our time running away from the real world, and you just can't get enough of it.

Anyway, I talked to my mom. She studied this stuff a lot more than my dad. You're right about all that stuff concerning Shiva. Even I could have told you most of that. But I found out something interesting about Ganesha—that's your elephant-headed guy. One of his titles—Hindu deities usually have infinite numbers of them—was "Lord of Obstacles" or some such. Apparently that means that if you don't behave, he puts obstacles on the path of your life, but if you do—proper worship of the gods and all—he can remove obstacles that keep you from that which you most desire.

Guess I should've prayed to him when I wanted Moira out of the way back in HS, huh? ;) Kidding! Actually, I've started seeing a guy out here just in the last week. His name is Drew, and he's pretty cool. All right, he's a muffin! (Yay, me!) Suddenly school isn't as bad as I thought it was.

Oh, before I forget, Mom talked to a friend of hers, trying to find out if there's some kind of ceremony all this stuff could be related to. They didn't know, but her friend's daughter goes to Harvard, and apparently, there's a professor there named Indira Arora who sort of wrote the book on ancient Hindu magick and stuff. You might want to look her up.

Love ya, kiss ya, already miss ya.

Priya

For several moments, Jenna just stared at her computer screen. Then she read the e-mail a second time, and a third. Her mind was racing. Somehow, with all of her personal issues clouding things, she'd let her interest in solving the puzzle of this case block out the real issue at hand: stopping the murderer before anyone else died as horribly as the Tyll girl.

Of course, with so little to go on, it had been easy to allow other things to cloud the issue. But now things had changed. It wasn't much of a lead, but it was something, an avenue to explore.

Quickly Jenna typed in a response to Priya.

Hey, Pri!
Way jazzed about your guy. Keep me posted. As the
levelheaded musketeer, though, I've gotta remind you
not to pin all your feelings about college on one guy.
That's just asking for trouble. Anyway, we'll hang
during the Turkey Day long weekend, and you can give
me the good dirt. Thanks so much for the help. Tell
your mom, too. I'll let you know if it pans out.
LYKYAMY,

J.

Jenna read the e-mail over once, then clicked Send.
She shut down the computer and picked up the phone.
In the top drawer of her desk, she found Danny Mariano's card, with his beeper number. She dialed it
quickly, listened to the long tone, and then hung up.

And waited.

While she sat there, someone knocked at her door.
Jenna jumped a bit, startled by the sudden invasion of
sound into the silence of her room. She crossed the
room quickly, glancing back at her phone. When she
opened the door, she found Damon Harris standing on
the other side.

"Hey," he said, offering a warm smile. "There's an
improv comedy thing over at the Campus Center at
ten. I was gonna head over. You want to come?"

Jenna glanced back at the phone, then back to Damon. She smiled, but distractedly.

"That'd be nice, Damon, but I can't tonight," she said. "I'm sorry."

He frowned, glanced away. When he looked back, Jenna thought he looked a little tired.

"Is this 'cause of Olivia?" he asked.

Jenna started to respond, but Damon held up both hands.

"Wait," he said. "Let me say my piece. I could tell that got you a little wacked the other night. Fine. But I'm not here to ask you on a date. We're friends. Maybe there could be more to it, maybe not. But I don't want not to hang with you just 'cause Olivia thinks I shouldn't date a white girl. Next thing she's gonna tell me I can't be friends with a person who's both white and female. Hell, Jenna, Olivia Adams is not my mother. You start worrying about what she thinks and you're playing into her whole race thing."

Jenna stared at him a second, realizing how right he was. Then she laughed, leaned forward and touched his hand.

"I really can't go tonight," she said. "But another night, definitely. Friends, great. And if something else comes out of it down the line . . ." She shrugged.

Damon nodded, then shrugged as well. "Besides, you've got your eye on that cop you keep talking about."

Jenna gaped at him, eyes wide. "What? Did Yoshiko . . . oh, never mind. Yeah, I like him, but he thinks I'm a kid.

And even . . . well, that's got nothing to do with you and me, or reality for that matter."

Damon gave her a sly grin. "Yeah."

Her phone rang.

"There's the call you're waiting for," Damon said. "I'll come by tomorrow. Maybe we can have lunch or something."

"Great," Jenna said, hearing the answering machine click on.

Damon walked back down the hall toward his room, and she shut the door quickly, then ran to grab the phone.

"Danny?" she said abruptly, without even a hello.

"What's going on?" he asked, and she liked the concern in his voice.

"You're gonna think it's crazy," she told him.

Saturday morning, at just past eleven o'clock, Jenna and Danny sat together in his car, which was parked on a tree-lined side street off of Mt. Auburn in Cambridge. With the sun glinting off the glass, they stared through the windshield at the three-story yellow Victorian across the street, sipping trendy flavored coffees from a nearby bakery and café called The Baked Bean.

The house was the property of Harvard University, and a number of faculty members had their offices there, including Professor Arora. According to the schedule she'd managed to get by calling Harvard, the professor had office hours from ten until noon on Saturday mornings, but so far, they hadn't seen anyone go in or out of the house.

They'd talked mostly about life since he'd picked her up an hour earlier. Jenna had told him about her father and Shayna, and a little about Hunter and Yoshiko, until she got the feeling it was more than he wanted to know. Or more personal than he wanted to get. Danny had shared a funny story about Slick that Jenna hadn't heard before, and then started talking about Audrey before clamming up suddenly.

So I'm not the only one who's noticed her attitude, she'd thought.

Now, after a prolonged silence, Danny sighed and glanced at Jenna. "This is crazy."

"Don't say I didn't warn you," she replied, without taking her eyes off the house across the street. "I have to say, though, if I'd known stakeouts were so boring, I'd have brought a book."

Danny raised an eyebrow. "What, my scintillating company isn't enough to keep you entertained?" He chuckled. "Actually, it is pretty boring, isn't it? We can't even be sure she's in there. We'll give it a couple more hours, and if she doesn't show, we'll call it a day, all right?"

Jenna smiled. For a guy she'd had to persuade to come along, he was being very cooperative. "Thanks," she said.

"For what?" he asked. "Not like I had anything to do today."

"You could have spent the day not being a cop," Jenna suggested.

"It's not something that goes away," Danny said, and

Jenna thought she sensed a bit of regret in his voice. "Okay, maybe I was reluctant, but now you've got me out here. I'm not gonna give up after the first hour."

Jenna smiled again, then turned to look back out the windshield. It hadn't been an easy thing, convincing Danny to give up part of his day off to follow her wild hunch. But, in some ways, Jenna was stunned that he'd agreed to it at all. She could only think of two reasons why he would have done that. Either he thought there was something to her suspicions, or he liked the idea of spending time with her. Since the latter idea was territory she'd already ventured into with him and found very awkward, she chose to think it was the former.

Just when she'd become comfortable with thinking that, he took another sip from his coffee, and then turned to her with an odd smile on his face.

"What?" she asked, squirming self-consciously.

"So you think this woman's our killer?" he asked dubiously.

Jenna shrugged. "I don't know what to think. All I know is, the one person in the Northeast who probably has a clue what this killer is trying to do just happens to be a woman who works right in the middle of the area where the murders have happened."

"Oh," Danny said, nodding, unsmiling. Then he turned to look at her again. "You're sure it wasn't just some ploy so we could go out on a date that wasn't really a date?"

Jenna's eyes went wide as she turned to stare at him. "What?" she demanded angrily. Then she saw that he wasn't being arrogant, as he'd sounded. Instead, the thin smile on his face as he tried not to laugh told her that he'd been teasing her.

Jenna didn't know which was better. She frowned and looked away. "That's not very funny."

"I'm sorry," Danny said, suddenly serious. "I guess I didn't mean that the way it sounded."

"Right," Jenna replied in a clipped tone. She felt herself blushing, her heart speeding up a bit, and hated herself for it. The air in the car suddenly seemed stifling. "Could you turn the engine on so I can roll my window down?"

He did as she asked, then looked back at her as she was putting the window down. "Jenna—"

"Know what? I'm embarrassed enough already. Could we change the subject?"

She kept her gaze locked on the house across the street. A moment later, however, she felt his strong hand on her shoulder, tugging gently. She turned to him.

Jenna sighed and shook her head, tension suddenly slipping away from her. *You can't run from this conversation,* she told herself.

"Look, Jenna," Danny started to say, "I'm sorry if—"

"No, stop," she said. "I'm sorry. I put you on the spot yesterday. Not only was it majorly not my style, but it was just dumb. I'm eighteen. Got it. I just thought there was something, I don't know, happening here."

She rolled her eyes.

"All right. I have a *crush* on you. Can't help it. And

maybe you're used to it. Whatever. I'll get over it. We can get back to reality. And no, that's not why I dragged you out here."

For a moment, they didn't look at one another. Danny raised his eyebrows and took a deep breath, then let it out. When he looked back at Jenna, she could see him out of her peripheral vision, but still couldn't face him.

"I didn't really think that," he said, then hesitated. "I . . . I guess I was flirting."

Surprised at his admission, Jenna looked up at Danny.

"See, I have a crush on you, too," he said quietly.

She stared at him a minute, then smiled, and even laughed a little. "I guess I look stupid with my mouth hanging open like that."

"No," he told her, eyes searching hers.

Danny reached out to stroke her cheek, and Jenna backed off a bit at first, and then allowed his fingers to caress her face. Her heart started to thunder in her chest and she felt as if she couldn't breathe. This wasn't at all what she had envisioned, or ever expected. In that moment, she wanted very badly to kiss him.

"I do have a crush on you," he said again.

Then he dropped his hand to his lap, and glanced away a moment. When he looked back at her, his expression was sad. "But you're right," he said. "You're eighteen. I don't think of you as a kid, that's for sure. You're more adult than most of the women I've dated. But it just . . ."

He let his words trail off.

"Wouldn't look right," Jenna finished for him.

Danny nodded. "I know how that sounds," he said. "But with my job, and the delicate personal relationships we all have to rely on every day . . . I mean, I don't think I could count on the same level of respect from my peers, or my lieutenant, or even from Slick. Especially Slick. They'd all think I was taking advantage of you or something. As if anyone could."

Jenna rolled her eyes at the compliment. Then she nodded slowly. "I understand," she said at length. "Really. I'd have to be wicked stupid not to notice the way Audrey gives me the evil eye now."

Again, a moment of silence. Then Danny spoke up. "You okay?" he asked.

"Yeah," she shrugged, trying to pretend that her attention was really on the house across the street. "I mean, I can still have a crush on you, right? I'm a big girl. A crush doesn't mean I'm gonna be heartbroken. I don't fall in love with a guy I've never even been out with. Besides, I've kind of been seeing someone off and on, anyway."

"Really?" Danny blinked in surprise. And maybe, Jenna secretly hoped, a little bit of jealousy.

"Yeah, it's pretty casual so far. But he's sweet."

"Huh. Well, good for you," he said awkwardly.

Jenna raised her eyebrows and stared out through the windshield. "Hey," she said. "Check it out."

Danny turned to see what had caught her attention. A woman had just stepped out the front door of the

Victorian, and Jenna was pretty certain it was Professor Arora. She was maybe a couple of inches over five feet tall, with shining brown skin. Jenna would have guessed her age to be midthirties, but she could have been older.

"Well, at least we'll get some exercise," Danny said.

They watched the woman walk up toward Mt. Auburn Street for half a minute. Then Jenna reached for the door handle, just as Danny started up the car.

"What are you doing?" she asked.

"Following her," Danny suggested.

Jenna narrowed her eyes. "You're not taking this seriously, are you? We'll never be able to tail her effectively in a car if she's on foot, and you know it."

"*Tail* her?"

"All right, I read too many books. But still."

He killed the engine. "You're right. We came out here. We'll do this the right way. But I still say you're taking a big shot in the dark."

Jenna smiled. "So are you, mister. You're here, aren't you?"

Shaking his head, Danny slipped an eight-by-ten card identifying him as a Somerset police officer onto the dash—Jenna figured that was to avoid getting towed—and then the two of them got out of the car and started hustling up the street toward Mt. Auburn. At the corner, Jenna spotted Professor Arora making her way toward Harvard Square, and they set off after her.

"So, how 'bout those Red Sox?" Jenna asked.

Danny frowned. "Um, I bet they're enjoying the off season."

Jenna rolled her eyes. "I knew that," she said. "Just making conversation. Trying to be inconspicuous. I know you're going to say someone like Professor Arora probably wouldn't notice if she was being followed 'cause she'd have no reason to think anyone would follow her. But if she's—"

"The killer," Danny finished. "Yeah. Got it. Y'know, Jenna, I'm a homicide detective. Some of this stuff I can figure out myself."

Jenna chuckled. "Good," she said. "I was sort of getting tired of having to hold your hand."

Danny glared at her playfully.

"So," Jenna said, still keeping her eye on Professor Arora. "Tell me about Kim."

"She didn't want to be with a cop," he replied. "So that was that. Anything more detailed you'd like to ask about, Miss Nosy?"

She laughed and bumped him with a shoulder, pushing him across the sidewalk. "All right, then," she replied, "tell me about Audrey. She was your mentor in homicide, but it can't have been easy for her getting to that point, as a woman I mean."

"That's for sure," Danny replied.

As they followed the professor, both trying to appear as disinterested as possible in her even as they watched her every step, Danny talked about his partner. Audrey Gaines had indeed had a difficult time getting to where she was. Even the city of Boston, which one would think of as progressive, had only had a couple of female homicide detectives in its history. And fewer black ones. She'd never married, and had apparently given up thinking about it. She had recently quit smoking for perhaps the tenth time, and was bitter about it.

"So what you're saying is, she's a generally cranky individual," Jenna said, as they followed the professor through Harvard Square and down toward the river.

"I didn't say that," Danny protested, but he was trying not to laugh. "She's a great cop."

"Doesn't mean she isn't cranky," Jenna replied archly.

Danny just sighed and shook his head. They kept walking. So did the professor. A couple of minutes went by, and then the half smile Jenna had been wearing disappeared completely from her face.

"Oh God," she whispered.

"What?" Danny asked, worriedly.

"You realize where we're headed, don't you?"

Danny looked back at the professor, who had stopped at the corner of Memorial Drive, waiting to cross at the light. Waiting to walk over to the park that ran alongside the Charles River.

They slowed, keeping their distance as the professor waited for the light to change.

Danny shook his head. "Nah, Jenna, come on," he said. "The woman works here. So she's walking down to the river. It's a sunny fall day. I'd walk down to the river, too, if I worked around here."

That last he didn't sound so sure about, Jenna thought.

"Maybe," she said.

"Maybe," Danny conceded.

Sure enough, though, as they continued to follow the professor, staying even farther behind as the other pedestrian traffic thinned out, she walked along the paved path beside the water, and when she reached the bridge under which the first murder had taken place, she veered from the path and started for the dark place under the bridge.

"You've got to be kidding," Danny muttered.

"What do you say now, smart-ass?" Jenna asked.

But Danny wasn't smiling. He grabbed Jenna's elbow and propelled her across Memorial Drive with him, dodging traffic. There, they sat on a low stone wall between some trees, and watched the darkness under the bridge, waiting for the professor to emerge.

"You shouldn't be here," he said after a minute or so had passed.

"You wouldn't be here if I hadn't called you," she reminded him.

Danny didn't speak again as they waited. Jenna had a million questions for him, but decided to keep quiet about them for the moment. Her hunch had just become something much more complicated.

"No way!" Yoshiko said. "You've gotta be kidding me. I mean, don't tell me you weren't surprised. Talk about wild guesses."

Jenna gave a small shrug. "It wasn't that wild a guess. But I was definitely surprised. It was a little too convenient, no question. I have to kind of wonder if she knew we were following her."

"That doesn't make sense, though," Yoshiko said. "Why would she give herself away like that?"

"Not much makes sense here," Jenna admitted. "Not unless Danny and I just got wicked lucky."

They were sitting together on the carpet in the middle of their dorm room, eating Chinese delivery and just enjoying each other's company. Hunter was out with some of his buddies, and Jenna was glad. It was nice just to hang with Yoshiko, doing the roomie thing.

Digging into her General Tsao's chicken, Yoshiko shook her head, chuckling softly. "I still can't believe you asked Danny out."

"Crush."

"This is Massachusetts," Yoshiko replied. "I haven't lived here that long, but I already know the insanity defense never works here."

Jenna laughed.

"Gotta say, though, the fact that he admitted he's got a crush on you, too . . . prodigiously cool."

"It was kind of . . . okay, yes, phenomenally cool," Jenna said, laughing. "Even though there's no future in it. I'm okay with that, though, I think. Maybe it'll help me put things into better perspective."

Yoshiko narrowed her eyes. "Why do I feel like we're talking about Damon?"

Jenna shrugged.

"Coy woman," Yoshiko scowled.

Their laughter was interrupted by the ringing of the phone. Jenna rose and went to answer it. Danny was on the other end of the line, and she listened carefully to what he had to say, her smile disappearing and a flush of pink rising to her cheeks.

Yoshiko saw her expression.

"What's up?" she asked worriedly, after Jenna had hung up.

"Just abject humiliation," Jenna replied numbly. "Nothing to be overly concerned about."

"Would you mind translating from subconscious to the rest of the world?"

Jenna met Yoshiko's questioning gaze.

"Professor Arora apparently had a very good reason for visiting the scene of the crime," she said, shaking her head and sighing.

"What?" Yoshiko cried in disbelief.

"She's working as a consultant for the Cambridge police," Jenna said flatly. Then she laughed, but there was no humor in it. "I just can't wait to face Slick and Dyson on Monday."

On Sunday morning Jenna borrowed her father's car and headed west on the Massachusetts Turnpike, to her home in Natick. It was another sunny day, the perfect, crisp kind of fall day that made her love New England. Thanks partially to the weather, and to the fact that her father's car had a compact disc player—she was cranking the volume on her Alana Davis CD and singing along to "32 Flavors"—she was beginning to put her embarrassment behind her.

Okay, it sucks. Reminds me of those dreams I had when I was a kid about showing up at school in my underwear.

But it'll keep till tomorrow.

And it *would* keep. For now, all she wanted to think about was her mother's birthday. April Blake had turned forty-seven the previous Thursday. Jenna had called and sent a card, but there was no way she was going to let it all go by without making a deal out of it. That just wasn't the way the Blake women did things.

Jenna was still singing along, five cuts deep into Alana Davis, when she guided her father's car off the Pike at Exit 13. She fished into the cup holder for some change to pay the toll, then headed down Route 30 to Speen Street, which took her deep into the heart of Natick.

It hadn't been that long since Jenna was home. Just a few weeks, really. But ever since she had moved away to college, every homecoming seemed something of an event to her. She was grown up now. This was the place she'd done all that growing, her hometown, but she'd moved on.

The world had moved on, as she'd read somewhere. And Jenna was moving along with it. And yet, coming home gave her a great deal of pleasure. As she drove through Natick, she let her eyes graze familiar stores and parks, and she imagined that at any moment she might see someone she knew. But most of the people she might recognize, the kids her age, had also moved on.

Jenna smiled as she sang.

Then the oddest thing happened. As she drove she noticed that a building on the right-hand side of the road—a convenience store that had stood there as long as she could remember—was being torn down.

That's not right, she thought.

But she'd thought it herself a moment earlier. The world was moving on. It was the first time she'd ever cared about something like that—a building being torn down in her town—and it wasn't exactly the most nostalgic of structures. But just as she'd felt that Somerset University was somehow *hers* now, seeing the rubble on the side of the road made her realize that Natick didn't really belong to her anymore. Or whatever part of it that had been hers was in the past now, just a memory.

Jenna then had a thought that made her laugh. *Growing up sucks.*

But she didn't really believe it.

A few minutes later she pulled into the driveway at 44 Knight Road. Her mother's house—the house she'd grown up in—looked the same at least. It was a big old colonial that needed to be painted. Jenna's mom, April Blake, was a surgeon, and could easily afford to pay to have the place painted. It was just a matter of getting around to picking up the phone and getting it done. Jenna would have to badger her about it, she realized.

As she walked up the front walk, she heard an odd sound from around the side of the house. It took her a second to recognize it, and then she smiled. Her mother liked to do yard work, whenever the hospital set her free for a while. When she walked around to the right of the house, where large maple trees dotted the property and filled much of the backyard, Jenna found her mother using a long, weathered old steel rake to drag leaves into large piles.

"Just getting around to it, huh?" Jenna asked.

April beamed. "Oh, hi honey," she said, and she met Jenna halfway for a hug and kiss. Then she gestured around them at the yard. "I thought I should get rid of all this before winter gets here. If the snow piles up on all these leaves—"

"It could kill the grass," Jenna finished for her. "So you've always said. But I never found out if that's a fact or just an urban legend or something."

"You doubt your mother?" April asked, arching one eyebrow.

"It's my job," Jenna replied. "I'm in college."

"Don't remind me. I know how old I am, thank you very much."

They hugged again. "Happy birthday, Mom," Jenna said. "Did you get my card?"

"Yes!" April replied. "Those tickets were too expensive, Jenna."

"Well, you missed *Rent* the first couple of times. I wanted to make sure you got to see it this time around," Jenna told her. "And you're worth it. Now go get cleaned up for lunch, will ya?"

"Wow, big spender," April said, putting the rake up on her shoulder and linking arms with her daughter as they walked toward the front of the house. "I'm going to have to tell Dr. Slikowski that he's paying you far too much."

"Would you feel better if I let you pay for lunch?" Jenna asked.

"Yes."

"Well, forget it."

They ate at a little Italian place called La Cantina, in the old part of Framingham. It had been a favorite of theirs for a long time, and Jenna vaguely remembered going out to lunch there when she was very small with both her parents. The clearest of those memories was of an entire herd of runners going by them while her father spooned minestrone soup into her mouth from a take-out container. La Cantina was along the Boston Marathon route, but back then she didn't really understand what all the running was about.

Jenna didn't have that many memories of her parents together. Most of the ones she did have weren't that pleasant. So she cherished La Cantina, even if she didn't really like minestrone soup. Though she connected her memory of the restaurant with her father, over the years she and her mother had gone there often enough on special occasions, and it had become *their* place.

Once upon a time, the restaurant had been a dark little hole in the wall. In recent years, it had been renovated into a classy little Italian paradise. Jenna had never been anywhere she could find food so good and pay so little. Whenever they went there, she ate too much, and that afternoon was no exception.

"This is so good," she said between bites of her meal, which consisted mainly of ziti, chicken, broccoli, some kind of cream, and more garlic than God had ever intended a human being to consume.

"Just don't kiss anyone later," her mother replied, laughing, and offered her another piece of freshly baked bread.

"Don't have anyone to kiss," Jenna confessed.

"Well, no wonder, spending all your time with dead guys," April teased.

Jenna just rolled her eyes. "Happy birthday, Mom."

April smiled. "Thanks, honey."

On the way home Jenna kept the radio on and sang along to every bubblegum pop song that she could find by punching her Dad's preselected channel buttons, the kind of stuff that she wouldn't have been caught dead listening to in her dorm. The time with her mother had left her in a good mood, and she didn't want that to go away. In a sense she knew she was hiding from the feelings that returning to Somerset would bring out of her.

Primary among these was dread.

The next day was Monday, and she had to go to work after classes. The idea of seeing Slick and Dyson, who would most certainly know what had happened, made her squirm. It was an honest mistake—Danny had been convinced enough to call the Cambridge police, asking that they bring Professor Arora in for questioning. And now they had both been terribly embarrassed. Danny more so, because this was his job.

Jenna didn't want to think about the things Audrey must have said when she realized that, for all intents and purposes, Danny had been on a stakeout with her. It was either tell the truth, or say they'd been on a date or something, which would be worse. No, the truth would have to do, embarrassing as it was.

That night Jenna did not sleep very well.

*　　*　　*

In the morning, she felt a kind of nervous energy that kept her going. It was only after her IR class let out that afternoon and she was on her way over to Slick's office that she began to feel tired again. *Ironic*, she thought. This was the time when she ought to have been the most anxious, and finally her fitful sleep from the night before was catching up with her.

Or maybe she'd just run out of energy to devote to her embarrassment.

When she stepped into the office, she was met with a blast of music, the freeform sounds of Charlie "Bird" Parker's horn. Dyson was there, just slipping into a white coat, and as Jenna walked in, he raised his eyebrows and smiled at her, shaking his head.

"Hey," Jenna said sheepishly.

"Well, if it isn't Dr. Watson," Dyson said in a bad English accent. "Holmes has been waiting for you, Watson. Seems you've bungled it this time."

Jenna frowned. "That's not funny."

He smiled. "I'm sorry, Jenna. It just struck me, y'know?" Dyson said quietly, so Slick couldn't hear him over the jazz. "He's kind of a control freak, you know? He's not used to people acting on impulse. As far as the cops are concerned, I think they're just annoyed that you're actually trying to do their job. It implies that they can't do it right—and in this case, they don't seem to be able to do much at all."

"I'm glad my life brings you so much amusement," she told him, but Jenna couldn't help a nervous smile.

"It'll be okay," Dyson promised. Then he went past her toward the door.

"Wait!" Jenna cried, panicked. "Where are you going? You're not gonna just leave me here."

Dyson lifted his hands in apology. "They're short in hematology. I promised I'd help out. What can I do?"

Jenna left the panicked, pleading look on her face, hoping it would keep Dyson from leaving. But it didn't do any good. He offered a tiny wave and was out the door. When he'd gone, Jenna turned to face the half-open door of Dr. Slikowski's inner office. Charlie Parker's horn did a wild kind of musical dance, and Jenna considered just turning and walking out.

After a moment, though, she shook her head firmly; she strode across the carpet to Slick's door and knocked twice. The music was turned down almost instantly.

"Come in."

She pushed the door open and stepped into the medical examiner's office. Though she knew she had followed a decent hunch, and the irrational defensive part of her argued that just because Professor Arora was working with the police didn't mean she wasn't the killer, Jenna felt a flush of embarrassment on her cheeks.

"I guess you wanted to see me," she said.

Dr. Slikowski leaned back in his wheelchair and regarded her carefully. He did not smile.

"Please, Jenna," he said, "have a seat."

She took the chair opposite his desk, and watched as he removed his wire-rimmed glasses and cleaned them gently with a cloth. After he'd slipped them back on, he peered at her carefully.

"You know, of course, what has come of your surveillance of Indira Arora," he began. When Jenna nodded, Slick continued. "Officially, Detective Mariano has played off his inquiry into the professor quite well, and it looks as though he was following a legitimate course of investigation."

Jenna frowned and started to protest, but Slick held up a hand.

"Which he was," the M.E. continued. "And, as you're an employee of this office, there's certainly no official problem with the fact that the two of you were working together in that regard."

"But unofficially . . ." Jenna said, feeling a bit ill.

"Unofficially, of course, Danny's getting a very hard time from his lieutenant and from his peers, and you can be certain the Cambridge police are going to be merciless."

"You talked to him?" Jenna asked, surprised.

"Not actually, no," Slick replied. "I spoke to Detective Gaines."

"I'm sure she's first in line at the stoning," Jenna muttered.

She was unprepared for the flash of anger that came over Dr. Slikowski's face.

"Why shouldn't she be?" he asked sharply. "Danny is her partner. She was unaware of his actions this past Saturday. He should have told her what he was involved in."

"He didn't take me seriously," Jenna argued. "He was probably just humoring me. Telling her would have meant that he believed there was something to what I was telling him."

Slick only looked at her sadly. "I wish you had shared your suspicions with me, Jenna. We're a team, after all. And if you have such little faith in your own instincts, perhaps you'll think twice about pursuing them at all in the future."

There was a long moment when only Charlie Parker made any noise. Then Jenna spoke up.

"I'm sorry, Dr. Slikowski. I didn't mean to embarrass you or anyone else. I know that the kinds of things I was getting involved in, following up beyond the walls of the M.E.'s office, really aren't what we do. It's just all so totally frustrating, realizing that there are things the cops won't take seriously . . . there are things I can contribute that they won't even listen to, because to them I'm just some little college girl. I'll try to keep my mouth shut and do my job."

When she looked up, she saw that Slick was staring at her incredulously and she became alarmed.

"Or do I even still have a job?" she asked quietly.

For the first time since she'd entered his office, Slick smiled. "Of course you do," he said, chuckling a bit. "You miss my point, Jenna. You're right, this job isn't about solving crimes. It's about finding the cause of someone's death. Sometimes, that means giving the police all the information we can provide them with so that they can solve a crime.

"But sometimes they ask for my help. And as far as I'm concerned, my help means the help of this office. You have a taste for this stuff, and a keen intellect, a real knack for seeing things other people might miss, or following a train of thought others might not ever even consider. I don't want you to stop doing that."

"You don't?"

"Not at all. But I don't want you to do it without involving me. Not ever. First of all, it's dangerous. Secondly, well . . . look at your friend Danny. He's in hot water because he went off on his own. I want you to work with me, Jenna, because I like working with *you*, and also because if we work together, no one will be able to question your actions."

Jenna didn't know what to say. Of all the possible outcomes from the embarrassment she'd felt on Saturday night, this one hadn't even occurred to her. Slowly, her expression changed from one of amazement to one of happiness.

"Thank you," she said. "And, Dr. Slikowski?"

He raised his eyebrows.

"I meant no disrespect, not coming to you," she said.

"I should have given you the space you needed," he replied. "Most people would have fired you, I suppose, but I love this sort of thing, the same way you do."

"Maybe love's too strong a word," she suggested.

"Oh, you don't see it that way," he argued. "You love all of this. Finding the truth."

"Solving the puzzle," Jenna echoed. "I guess that's true."

Slick leaned forward slightly. "The key, you see, is doing it all within the boundaries of authority. Not stepping on anyone's toes. For now, you can let me handle that, but pay attention."

"I will," she agreed.

"Excellent. Now get some work done; we have a visitor arriving shortly," he told her.

Curious, Jenna went to her desk and started keying in some of the records from recent autopsies. Twenty minutes later there was a knock on the door, and Jenna was astonished when Professor Indira Arora walked into the office.

"Uh, hi," she said awkwardly. "Can I help you?"

Professor Arora smiled kindly and identified herself. "I'm looking for Dr. Slikowski," she added.

Before Jenna could respond, Slick appeared in the doorway to his office. "I'm Walter Slikowski, Professor. Thank you for coming down."

"I confess I was intrigued, Doctor," the professor replied. "I have never been asked to consult with the police before. Though I gather you're used to such things."

"Unfortunately, this isn't the first time the police have needed the assistance of this office," Slick replied diplomatically. "And I doubt it will be the last. Won't you come in?"

As he spoke, Dr. Slikowski wheeled his chair backward into his office to allow the professor room to enter. Then he looked at Jenna and offered an enigmatic smile.

"Jenna, would you join us, please?"

For a moment she didn't reply. She was more than a bit startled by the request. Unless it was because Slick wanted to upbraid her in the presence of the professor, so as to at least give the appearance that she had been chastised for her irresponsible behavior. With a sigh, Jenna walked into the M.E.'s office. Light jazz piano music drifted from the speakers at very low volume. There were two chairs in there, and Professor Arora was already sitting in one of them.

Jenna might have taken the other if the professor hadn't turned around to stare at her as she entered.

"So you're Jenna?" the woman said. "I suppose I should have guessed that. You know, I've never been, what would the term be, staked out? I've never been staked out before. It was fascinating, in a way."

"I'm so sorry, Professor," Jenna replied. "It's just . . . I didn't know, and when you went down to the river, I thought—"

Professor Arora waved her concerns away. "Of course you did. Don't worry about it, really. Actually, I'd be interested in hearing all about the train of thought that led you to keep an eye on me, so to speak. It was certainly interesting to find out that someone, somewhere, thought I might be a murderer."

Jenna stared at her. Then she shook her head in disbelief. "I think you're taking it pretty well," she said. "I really am sorry, though."

"Not at all," the professor said, and her tone let Jenna know that was the end of it. Then she turned back to Slick. "So, shall we get down to business?"

They spoke briefly about the police investigation, particularly into the ashes that were found on the body. There seemed to have been no progress on that front. Slick explained Jenna's theory that the killer was a woman, and how she had come by that theory.

"How do you stand on that issue, Dr. Slikowski?" Professor Arora asked.

"Walter, please," Slick replied.

"And I'm Indira," she added, smiling.

Slick nodded. "While I do not discount the possibility that the killer is a man, I am inclined to agree with Jenna, both on the strength of the physical factors we've observed, and on instinct."

"Instinct, Walter? That's rather unscientific for a man in your field, isn't it?" Indira asked.

For some reason, Slick smiled warmly at Jenna. "All creatures have instinct. In pathology and forensics, yes, of course you're right. We deal in observable phenomena. But when you want to solve a crime, sometimes you have to go on instinct." He glanced back at Indira. "Of course, we're not detectives."

Indira smiled thinly and tilted her head slightly at that, but made no comment. After a moment she turned to Jenna.

"So," she said. "Instinct. Is that what led you to me?"

"Well, half that and half logic," Jenna said, still feeling as though she was apologizing. "It just seemed to me that while everyone knew that the symbols involved with the murders were Hindu, nobody knew what their significance was, apparently because whatever ritual they referred to is so old. Which meant whoever was killing these people had some kind of special knowledge.

"A friend of mine's parents recommended that I contact you—I guess the same way the Cambridge police did—and since you're a woman, and the right height, and you have the knowledge, and I didn't know if you had an alibi or not—"

"That made me a suspect," Indira finished for her. "Well, your thinking is certainly sound, Jenna. In fact, I don't really have a solid alibi for either of those nights. On the thirtieth, I was out of town, and the night of the second murder, I was home asleep. Nobody there but my roommate, whom I imagine was also sleeping. So there you have it. Instant suspect."

Jenna blushed a bit. "I'm not suggesting that—"

"Why not?" Indira laughed. "Maybe having me on their payroll is a way for the Cambridge cops to keep an eye on me, though I'm not sure they'd followed the same investigative logic as you, so we'll see. In any case, you're also right that I have the knowledge you were talking about."

Now it was Slick's turn to be taken off-guard.

"What's that?" he asked. "You know what these rituals are? No one told me that."

Indira nodded. "I think they're trying to keep it very quiet. As Jenna says, it's a specialized kind of knowledge. But the rituals are almost certainly meant to re-create a very crude, very archaic Hindu magick ceremony that was supposed to induce the transmigration of the soul."

"The huh?" Jenna asked.

"I'm sorry," Slick interjected. "Are we talking about reincarnation?"

"Not precisely," Indira replied. "Or, at least, not in this instance. Of course, Hinduism puts a great deal of faith in what you call reincarnation. But this ritual seems to have been created to force transmigration, the movement of the human soul from one vessel to another, without any stops in between, so to speak. To transfer one's entire self and consciousness from one body to another."

Jenna frowned. "So that's why the elephant man," she said. "The Lord of Obstacles, right?"

Indira smiled broadly. "Why, yes. Very astute. Shiva's power of the dead is part of the mythology, as is the power of the moon. Shiva's veins flow with the ashes of the dead, hence the ashes found on the bodies. Nothing in this kind of ancient ritual happens without supplication to Shiva. But Ganesha—your elephant man—actually serves a vital purpose to the ritual. Shiva might give the supplicant the blessing of transmigration, but there must be an empty vessel for him . . ." She paused to nod at Jenna. "Or her . . . to jump to. Ganesha's function is to remove the obstacle in question, namely the soul of the person whose form is being overtaken."

"That's not only a horrible thought, but patently impossible as well," Slick said dismissively. "You're talking about, what? Body hijacking?"

Indira nodded reasonably. "So it would seem. I'm not saying I believe in it, of course. It's an archaic bit of magick, Walter, not the kind of thing anyone has practiced in thousands of years. Although there are stories, from time to time. About twenty-five years ago, there was a young girl in Calcutta who'd suffered a massive head injury of some sort. She was completely catatonic. She remained that way for several weeks, until she woke up quite suddenly, with no explanation for her recovery. Save for one.

"When she awoke, she did not recognize any of her family members. In fact, she claimed to be someone else entirely, a middle-aged woman who had died several miles away just before the girl came back to her senses. According to all reports, the girl had all of the memories of the deceased woman, and none of the life she had led previous to the head injury she suffered."

Jenna felt tiny pinprick needles of ice all over her body. Then, almost as if he had read her mind, Slick cleared his throat a bit and sat up straighter in his chair.

"That's an eerie tale, certainly," he told Indira. "But we have no evidence that it actually happened, and even so, it doesn't prove—"

"No, you're right, of course," Indira added. "It doesn't prove a thing. As for evidence, however, you'll just have to take my word for it. You see, I've met the girl. Though she's a woman now."

Jenna saw that Slick had no reply for that, and she couldn't blame him. It was all a little overwhelming. Finally, she was the one who spoke up.

"And you've told the police all of this?" she asked.

"Oh, yes," Indira replied, smiling. "They weren't half so polite with their disbelief as you two have been."

"I thought you said you didn't believe all of this?" Jenna asked, surprised.

"That isn't quite what I said, but you're right. I suppose I don't really believe it. But as that little girl shows us, there are certainly those who do believe. Though I doubt many of them live on this continent."

"Couldn't the ritual be meant to cover up another motive?" Slick suggested.

Jenna looked at him a moment. "She went to some pretty amazing lengths if it's all just a cover-up. The ashes, for starters. And why, of all things, this? Aren't there simpler ways to throw police off your trail if that's your goal?"

"I'd have to agree," Indira added. "And let's not forget those Japanese characters the police found at the Kettle Square site."

"What?" Jenna asked, glancing from one to the other. "I didn't know about that? What characters?"

Slick raised his eyebrows. "I'm sorry, Jenna. With the immediacy of our conversation earlier, I'd forgotten to bring it up. In addition to the Hindu symbols, there were several ancient Japanese symbols, language characters, painted on the floor at the scene of Stephanie Tyll's murder."

"What were they?" Jenna asked.

"Apparently some sort of reference to a mythological figure called Izanagi. Detective Gaines is looking into it," Slick replied.

Silence again. Slick glanced from Indira to Jenna and back again.

"Just for a moment, let's suppose that this *is* our killer's goal," he offered. "If the murderer believes she'll be able to steal someone else's body in this way, that's all well and good. But what's the point? If the murder is not being committed out of rage or psychosis . . . let me begin again. Even if you could force someone's soul from his body and take it over, why would you want to do such a thing? It isn't vanity. If our killer is a woman, she'd have to be desperate to be so indiscriminate about her potential new 'vessel,' yes?"

The three of them considered that for a moment.

Then Jenna offered a small shrug.

"Maybe she's dying."

c h a p t e r   9

*M*oonlight.

She knew that's what she had missed the last time, with the girl in the restaurant in Somerset. She'd thought that by concerning herself with the netherworld more, through the worship of Izanagi, the moon would be unnecessary.

Stupid. A waste of time. I took a life for nothing.

It haunted her, to know that she had taken that girl's life without proper preparation. That wasn't what any of this was about. Not at all. The runner, that first night, he was a failed experiment. It was a shame that anyone had to die, but she had long since come to the realization that it was necessary.

For her to live, another must die.

But that young girl . . . without the moon, her death had been meaningless. And what had happened after her death . . . it was too much. She had been so enraged by her own stupidity that she had blamed the girl at first . . . had *punished* her, defacing the body that had been denied her. But it was not that poor girl's fault, and she knew that now.

She would have to attempt to contain her temper if there were other disappointments. It would not do to give the police too much to work with. It didn't matter if they discovered her identity after she had already transmigrated. By then, she would be another person entirely. But beforehand, she could not afford to be discovered.

I've got to be certain it will work. No more needless killing. One more death, and that will do it. I'll have the body I need. The future. The life. Only one more.

I've got to be certain.

And she was certain. Her research had made it clear to her what she was missing. If Ganesha could loose a soul from its moorings, that was one thing, but without somewhere for it to go, it seemed even the most powerful of gods could not banish it. She had found, in her studies, a terribly ancient bit of Gaulish magick that should help to guide the soul to the land of the dead. If this added spell worked, she had reasoned, it should expedite the departure of her victim's soul, and her goal might be accomplished.

Which was what had brought her here, tonight. The moon was not full, but it was very bright in the sky above. The stars infinite and clear. The wind brought a bitter chill, and she shivered, for she was not dressed for the weather. When the ritual took hold, when it finally worked, her body would be left behind. Though it had betrayed her in so many ways, she respected it enough that she wanted to present her body well, even in death.

In silence, she sat behind the wheel of the car at the far end of the parking lot beneath a small line of trees. Though the Charles River Park had been the perfect site for her purposes, she didn't dare return there. And there were so few appropriate places, spots that were isolated and yet where someone might happen by, that she had to look carefully for each site.

The last one had been a mistake.

The moonlight, she thought again, and slammed her fist hard against her thigh. Hard enough to leave a bruise. *Fool.* But this would be different. Tonight would be very different.

Tonight she would succeed.

She sat in the car and peered through the windshield, across the other cars in the lot, across the street, to the front door of Jah-Man. Reggae music poured from the building each time the door was opened. Many times, someone would pull into the lot, park, and go toward the club, or come out and get into their car and take off.

But the risk was too great.

So she stayed there, quite still, her mind humming along to the distant reggae beat. Eventually the music stopped. After a time the lot was almost entirely empty. There were four other cars besides her own. For the longest time, no one else came out, and she wondered if the other cars might not belong to local residents, parked illegally overnight in the lot.

Finally the door opened again. Two people came out together. A man and a woman. She cursed under her breath, furious that she might not be able to perform the ritual that night. Then she watched as the man walked the woman to one car, kissed her good night, and then walked to his own as the woman drove away.

She stepped out of her car.

"Excuse me?" she called, her voice containing just the right amount of fear and anxiety.

The man stared at her, then smiled reassuringly, to let her know that he wasn't a predator, to set her at ease. After all, it was dark in the lot, and she was a woman alone with a tall, powerful man.

She stepped out from behind her car door, to let him see her, to see the sheer dress, and her legs. And then she looked at him with what she knew were the most pitiful eyes.

Men were so stupid. And yet, so powerful. She would enjoy spending time as a man. And if she didn't like it . . .

I can always change back. Once I've mastered it, I can have any body I want.

"My car won't start," she said nervously. "Could you help me?"

He smiled confidently. "I'll see what I can do," he said, only a bit of the islands in his accent. "Why don't you pop the hood?"

"Oh. Sure," she said, giving him a vacant look. "How?"

Now he looked at her as though she were colossally stupid. For a moment, just a moment, she wondered if he would get it. If some primitive part of his brain would warn him that this was a trap, a snare set out for the most dangerous animal of all. But he was a man, after all. And she knew that she looked amazing in that dress.

"Here, I'll do it," he said, his voice an attempt to soothe her.

He stepped around the door and bent to reach under the dash. Which was when she lifted the taser and pressed it against the smooth flesh at the back of his neck. He grunted in pain and surprise, jerked a bit, and then fell, half in, half out of the car.

She dragged his body behind the car—she'd purposely parked a little too far out, to leave space where she had painted the symbols needed for the ritual. She tore open his shirt and admired the way the moonlight gleamed on his ebony skin. With the black marker, she drew the third eye on his forehead, then sprinkled the ashes onto his chest. With the skull she retrieved from the backseat of the car, she danced.

Then she killed him.

When the phone rang early Tuesday morning, and Jenna stumbled over, half asleep, to knock it from its cradle before actually managing to fumble it to her ear, she expected to hear the voice of one of her parents on the other end of the line. Or maybe Yoshiko's mother.

The last thing on earth she expected, though, was to hear the apologetic voice that actually was on the other end of the line.

"Jenna, I'm sorry to disturb you so early," Dr. Slikowski said. "I imagine you were sleeping."

Astonished, and still barely able to open her eyes, Jenna could only mumble her surprise.

"Slick?"

The moment she'd said it, her eyes went wide and she snapped awake. The medical examiner did not like his nickname, not at all. Jenna desperately tried to think of something to say.

"Jenna?"

"Oh, Dr. Slikowski," she said, scrambling. "It's you. I thought it was someone else. This friend. Who lives in England. He sometimes forgets the time difference and calls really early, and—"

"It's all right," he said, sounding more amused than she would have guessed. "Believe me, it's not the first time I've heard that nickname, and I'm not so arrogant that I don't appreciate the irony."

"I . . . I'm not sure I follow," she said, feeling somehow very guilty.

"You don't need to," he promised. "Just please don't call me that around the SMC staff."

"Cross my heart," she said. "I'm sorry." Then she remembered how early it was . . . *How early is it?* She looked at the clock and saw that it wasn't quite seven in the morning. "What's going on? Is something wrong?"

"Our would-be soul survivor," he explained, and let her take a moment for it to sink in.

"Another murder?" she asked.

"In Kendall Square," he confirmed. "I'm headed over

there now. I don't want to make you late for class, but it shouldn't take long, if you'd like to join me."

"I can be ready in fifteen minutes," she said quickly.

"I'll be there in twenty."

They parked just beyond the entrance to the parking lot, as most of the lot was filled with police cars. Jenna waited for Slick to lower his chair down from the van, and then the two of them went toward the line of police officers. There was a team with a camera from Channel 7, and that made Jenna nervous. She noticed a couple of uniformed cops glance her way, look at Slick, and then mutter something to each other that made them both laugh.

Much as it pained her to admit, she felt as though she didn't belong there. It didn't matter that both Slick and Professor Arora hadn't been really angry with her, her goof with the professor had embarrassed Danny and given the Cambridge cops something with which to taunt her.

You're taking this too personally, Blake, she told herself. But it didn't matter—she couldn't help it. Jenna took another look at the cameras, and without even asking, stepped behind Dr. Slikowski, grabbed the handles, and began to push him in the wheelchair.

He grabbed the wheels and forced them both to a stop.

"What are you doing?" he asked as casually as he was able, cognizant, just as Jenna was, that the Channel 7 camera was swinging their way.

"I'm sorry," she said, her voice low so the microphone couldn't pick it up. "I just thought if I pushed, they wouldn't question what I'm doing here. I know I'm not really supposed to—"

"First of all," he said, his voice also low, but very grave. "I will decide if you are supposed to be here. Your pushing me not only makes me look as if I need your help, an image I do not want to convey, but it also makes it appear as though that is the only reason you are with me, which is an image I should think you would not want to convey."

Jenna blinked, a bit hurt by his sharp tone. A moment later, she realized she deserved it. Not merely for her presumption—she knew he hated to have anyone push his chair—but for giving in to the attitude against her without even trying to deal with it.

When Slick moved on, Jenna walked by his side, but slightly back. He was the boss, no question, but he had brought her along, and that meant something. To her, and, she suspected, to the police as well, no matter how much they wanted to make fun of her.

And they did.

When he turned to see them coming across the lot, Detective Flannery grinned broadly. It wasn't a happy grin, or a kind one.

"Well, if it ain't Nancy Drew," he drawled.

Several of the officers around him chuckled. Slick shot Flannery a look that made the detective pretend to stifle his denigrating smile. But the M.E. said nothing.

"Nice to see you again, Detective Flannery," Jenna

said calmly. "It seems our killer's more comfortable in Cambridge, doesn't it?"

As Flannery puzzled over that one, Jenna pushed right past the police. Seeing that she was with Slick, and speaking to Flannery, no one moved to bar her passage, even for a moment. Then, as she moved by Flannery to get to the body, she paused to regard him.

"Maybe she figures it's easier to get away with homicide in your city," Jenna suggested.

The other cops laughed out loud at that one, though she'd actually insulted the entire lot of them. For his part, Flannery glared at her, nostrils flaring, but said nothing. Jenna told herself it was because he wasn't a clever man and couldn't think of anything to say. She tried not to consider that she might have made an enemy of a man she could need in the future, if she did pursue a career in pathology or forensics.

Jenna stepped out of the way, literally using her body to clear a path so Dr. Slikowski could wheel himself up to the crime scene. She lifted the police tape to let him pass under and followed him through.

On the other side of the tape, Slick paused and looked back at Flannery. "Joe, you people all through with tire tracks and such in here?" he asked.

Flannery nodded, but didn't smile. Jenna got the feeling that if it were up to Detective Flannery, Dr. Slikowski would no longer be a consultant on this case. Thankfully, however, the request for aid had come from much higher up than one homicide detective.

"You're all set," the man said grumpily. "My boys

have been in and out of there a million times. I'm sure they've tracked over any useful evidence by now."

Jenna was surprised by his candor, but only until she realized Flannery was making a joke aimed in her general direction. She'd insinuated that his squad were bumbling idiots, and Flannery was throwing it back at her. She almost laughed, but even though he'd made a joke, Flannery didn't seem like he'd want her to think it was funny.

"Let's have a look," Slick said quietly.

Jenna followed him over to where the still form of the murder victim lay beneath a dark sheet. Soon they'd be bagging him. For the moment it was just that sheet, and the white lines they'd drawn around his body. Slick nodded toward it, and Jenna stooped to pull the sheet back. She could feel numerous pairs of eyes burning into her back, as if she'd crossed some line. In a way she had. If Slick had been able to pull the sheet back himself, that would have been one thing. But she was just an assistant. To them, she was an outsider invading their crime scene.

"Well, what have we here?" Slick muttered under his breath.

Jenna realized she hadn't even looked at the dead man, so attuned was she to her surroundings. She refocused now, and what she saw gave her pause, and a bit of nausea as well.

The man had been strangled, that was easy to see from the ligature marks around his neck. But Jenna wasn't at all certain that the strangulation was what had killed him.

Nope. I'd be willing to bet it was that hole in his head.

"Whoa," Jenna whispered.

"What do you make of it?" Dr. Slikowski asked her, too quietly for anyone to hear, save for the uniformed officer standing just a few feet from the body. *Guardian of the dead, or something.*

Jenna looked at the hole, and the dried trickle of blood that had flowed from it. It was a very small hole, no more than a quarter of an inch across, and it had been forcibly punched through the dead man's skull right at the center of the eye that had been drawn in Magic Marker.

"She blew it again," Jenna said, though she wasn't quite sure if that made sense. "Got mad again. Only this time, she either controlled it better, or didn't have time to do more than this."

"Possibly," Slick replied. "But if we take Indira Arora's theory, and presume that the addition of Japanese mysticism at the last murder is evidence that the killer is, shall we say, improvising, trying to come up with the right confluence of elements . . . Maybe she was simply trying to make herself a way in."

Jenna frowned. "But that doesn't make sense," she said. "I mean, you punch something through the skull, chances are the body's not going to be any good to you if you do manage to steal it." Then she shook her head. "And I can't believe we're having this conversation."

Slick smiled grimly. "Nevertheless." He paused. "Have you ever heard of trepanning?"

Jenna drew a blank.

"It's the practice of drilling a hole in a skull in order to release pressure. Some people believe it lets evil spirits out. That is among several colorful explanations that have been given for it. Usually it is self-inflicted and the aim of the wound is a bit more . . . strategic."

With an odd look, Jenna moved closer to him. "You think this is funny?" she asked in a horrified whisper.

"Not at all," he replied. "But I'm baffled. I don't react well to bafflement. It usually brings out a certain levity in me."

"I'm sure that's helpful," she said sarcastically.

"Not really, no."

Then Flannery came up behind them, hitching up his pants. "So what do you think, Walt?" he asked. "Gotta be an ice pick, maybe an awl. Maybe a good-size spike. Guy must've used a hammer or a rock to drive it, but we didn't find any tools around."

"Or any suspicious rocks, eh?" Dr. Slikowski asked, then smiled thinly at Flannery to let the detective know it was a good-natured joke, not a taunt. "In any case, Joe, you know better than to ask me something like that before the autopsy."

Flannery nodded. "All right. Call me when you're done?"

"Of course," Slick replied. "I presume we had the usual artistic elements, the Shiva symbols?"

"Right over there," Flannery said, and pointed to the edge of the lot under the branches of a line of trees.

Jenna and Slick went to look at the symbols. They were the same as before—Shiva, Ganesha, and the moon-and-skull combination—and Jenna glanced around for the additions Slick had told her about.

"Where's the Japanese stuff?" she asked.

Flannery heard her and shrugged. "I saw the pictures from the Somerset victim. We didn't have anything like that."

Jenna heard hesitation in his voice. "But?" she asked.

Flannery pointed to where someone had made a circle of stones in the lot. Jenna had seen it when they'd first walked up, but assumed that somebody had built a fire there. That's what it looked like to her, the kind of little fireplace a camper might build in the woods. But when they walked over to look at it, she saw that it was anything but that. Inside, there was a drawing.

"Is that chalk?" Slick asked.

"Yeah. The photographer got pictures, so don't worry about messing it up," Flannery said. "And before you ask, we looked at the rocks on top. I don't think any of these was used to drive whatever it was into the deceased's head."

The chalked image was a male figure with a long beard—an old man, she figured—carrying a large club. He had a very long tongue, which hung out of his mouth, and there were what appeared to be strings or chains that ran from his tongue to either ear.

"Why use paint over there and chalk over here?" Jenna asked.

"My guess would be the killer needed to be more specific in this bit than in the painted stuff. Something about the drawing," Flannery replied.

Jenna was surprised, not merely because his answer made a great deal of sense, but because he had bothered to respond to her at all. She decided not to make a big deal out of it, though, and only nodded thoughtfully in reply. It was a habit she was picking up from Slick.

"We also found some kind of seeds in there," Flannery added, nodding toward the stone circle. "Oh, and the tongues."

He said this last so offhandedly that Jenna wasn't certain she'd heard him right. When she saw that he was smiling again, she knew that she had.

"Tongues?" Slick asked, and Jenna was glad it was him and not her.

"Cow, we think," Flannery replied. "We've sent those and the seeds off to the lab."

There was a little more conversation after that, but Jenna could barely pay attention. Her mind had gotten pretty much stalled on the word *tongues*.

To Jenna's surprise, Slick didn't bring up her gaffe, or Flannery's attitude, the entire ride back to Somerset. He offered to drop her at her class, but she was so late for American lit she decided she'd be better off not going at all than showing up half an hour after the class had begun. Instead, she had him drop her at the dorm so she could hook up with Hunter and Yoshiko for lunch before heading off to her European history class.

"Thanks for coming along," Slick said, as she stepped down from the van.

"Thanks for asking," she replied earnestly. "I was

pretty mortified over what happened. I guess I just got to thinking I knew better than everyone else. I felt like an idiot, and I knew Flannery wasn't going to cut me any slack."

"Neither is Audrey Gaines when you see her," Slick confirmed.

"Great. I'll look forward to it," Jenna said sheepishly.

"You can take it," he told her. "This morning proved that, didn't it?"

She thought about that for a second. "Yeah. I guess it did," she said. Then she looked at him closely. "Thanks, Dr. Slikowski. For everything."

He only smiled. Jenna went to shut the door, but he called her name and she pulled it back open and looked at him expectantly.

"I know that ancient Hindu mythology is Professor Arora's specialty, but maybe she could give us some idea about the Japanese angle, not to mention whatever that was in the lot today. I suppose it's possible it was Hindu, but it seemed very out of place."

"I thought so too," she said. "Instinct."

Slick nodded. "Instinct. When you have a few moments, even if it's not until you come to work tomorrow, why don't you give her a call."

"Sure," Jenna said. "No problem."

When Slick pulled away in the van, and Jenna started walking around toward the front of the dorm, she smiled to herself.

Girl with a mission.

chapter 10

After history class that Tuesday afternoon, Jenna went back to her room to catch up on some of the work she'd been been lagging behind on. In particular, she had been avoiding biology for about a week and needed to do her assigned reading. She spent a couple of hours with her nose in the book, and then read over the notes she'd taken in class on Friday and Monday, trying to make sense of them in light of the assignments. She knew that if she could get it straight in her head, she'd have an easy time studying it all later.

Eventually, she found herself growing sleepy, her eyelids drooping, and she knew that she'd managed all the studying that was going to happen that afternoon. She had some biographical research to do on Jack London for an American lit paper, and decided to head over to the library to see what books she could find. She'd been tempted, actually, to write about Herman

Melville and *Moby Dick*, pretty much because she hated the damned book and wanted to share her ire. But then she'd seen on the curriculum that a separate course was offered specifically on Poe, Hawthorne, and Melville and decided to hold off until next semester.

Yawning and stretching, she pulled her shoes back on and picked her jacket up off the back of her desk chair. Then she paused a moment, realizing there was something she'd meant to do.

"Professor Arora," she reminded herself.

It could have waited until the next day, but Jenna felt as if she needed to impress the woman somehow. She'd made an idiot out of herself in front of the professor and wanted to erase that image, even though the woman insisted that she wasn't bothered by it at all.

She dialed the main number for Harvard University and asked to speak with Indira Arora. A few seconds later, she was connected to the professor's office. The phone rang on the other end, and Jenna prepared to leave a message. Her father was a professor, and she knew that other than posted office hours, they were generally either in class or at home, so she was surprised when Indira answered the phone.

"Indira Arora," the woman said.

"Hello, Professor, this is Jenna Blake. We met yesterday?"

"Of course, Jenna, I remember," Indira replied.

Jenna thought she heard some amusement in the woman's voice, and decided that was preferable to anything else.

"I guess you spoke to Dr. Slikowski about the murder last night," Jenna began. "He asked me to call to see if you had any leads regarding the Japanese and other rituals that are being incorporated into the killer's M.O."

The professor actually laughed. "I'm sorry, Jenna," she said, sighing. "All of this just sounds so foreign to me. Leads, M.O., that sort of thing. Does it ever make you self-conscious, talking like that?"

Jenna chuckled as well. She liked the professor's forthrightness. Indira seemed to say just what was on her mind, though Jenna wondered if she'd draw the line if what she had to say was unkind.

"Sometimes, I guess," she admitted. "But when you've been in on an autopsy, you tend to take it more seriously."

"Of course," Indira said gravely. "I don't mean to be disrespectful of the victims, you understand."

"Absolutely," Jenna reassured her, uncomfortable now because Indira herself seemed uncomfortable. "Anyway, I know you've probably been talking nonstop to the police, and it's a bit out of bounds, even though he's been asked to consult, but Dr. Slikowski has taken an interest in this case, and I guess he was—"

There was some kind of disruption on the other end of the phone, and Jenna stopped talking. After a moment, Indira came back on.

"I'm sorry, Jenna, I have to go. I don't know how much help I can be, but I'm happy to talk to you about it. Would you like to come by the house later? I'm actually not far from you, just outside Porter Square. That's barely a T stop away. I might have some books in my library that would be a place for you to start."

"That would be great," Jenna replied instantly. She liked the idea of making a good impression on Indira, as well as bringing back some books that might help her and Slick in their research. "What time?"

Professor Arora suggested seven o'clock, and even though Jenna knew she had a sorority party to go to later, she agreed. She'd just have to be fashionably late. Indira gave her directions, and they hung up.

Jenna scrawled a quick note to let Yoshiko know that she'd meet her at the party, and then she was off to the library.

Professor Arora's house really was close to Porter Square. In fact, it was just off Massachusetts Avenue on a side street where the main landmark was a dingy-looking restaurant with the testosterone-laced sobriquet of "Nick's Beef and Beer." As she walked past Nick's, Jenna had to wonder if a woman had ever set foot in the place.

On the other hand, I'm sure there are plenty of women who like beef and beer a damn sight more than I do.

The professor lived in the fifth house on the left, a boxy two-story colonial that had long since lost its shine. It was a nice-looking house, and from what she could see in the light of the street lamps, she guessed that it had been freshly painted. Unfortunately, the paint was a kind of dull beige, which didn't suit the style of the place, and the yard needed some serious landscaping, something a woman as busy as Indira Arora would never do.

The night was cold, and Jenna huddled inside her leather jacket for protection as she went up the front steps. The doorbell chimed loud and clear from inside the house. There was a row of small windows beside the door, with a curtain tied across them, but she could see a bit of the house. Gleaming hardwood floors, warm lights, antique furniture. Apparently the professor made time to take care of the inside of the house.

The sound of footsteps on the wood floor reached her, and then Jenna heard the dead bolt being pulled back. When the door opened, she was greeted by the face of a stranger, a dark-haired woman with deep-red lips parted in a warm and welcoming smile.

"Oh, I'm sorry—"

"You must be Jenna," the woman interrupted. "Come on in."

She stepped out of the way and Jenna entered the house.

"Indira!" the woman called. "You have company!" Then she turned to Jenna, very amused. "I'm sorry. I just got such a kick out of her being a murder suspect, even for half a second."

Jenna blushed a bit and glanced away. Then Indira came down the stairs, wearing blue cotton pants, sneakers, and a Harvard sweatshirt. Every time Jenna saw her, the woman surprised her a little more.

"Jenna, meet Carol Westling. She's an English professor at Harvard, my roommate, and an all-around pain in the neck," Indira said, glaring at her roommate.

"Nice to meet you," Jenna said.

Carol laughed. "You too. I'm headed out, actually, but make yourself at home. Indira actually knows how to make tea, despite what she may pretend."

There was a brief flurry of activity as Carol slipped into a jacket, vowed to bring back some groceries, and then slipped out the door. Jenna took the opportunity to look around a bit. There was a fireplace, with some really interesting-looking art—which she assumed was Indian—above the mantel. There were two antique tri-cornered chairs, one on either side of a maple entertainment center, an array of plants and vases, and several beautiful carpets. She also noticed a bookcase filled with old volumes, and hoped she'd have a chance to look at some of them.

"Shall we, Jenna?" Indira asked, and Jenna followed her into the kitchen. "What about that tea? Do you even drink tea, or is it purely coffee for you, like most college students?"

"I'd love a cup of tea," Jenna assured her. Then, while the water was heating in the kettle, she got down to business. "I don't want to take up too much of your time, Professor—"

"Indira, please."

"Indira," Jenna nodded. "But if there's anything or anyone you can think of who might be able to help us figure out the significance of all this, we'd appreciate it."

"Actually," Indira said, "I got home a bit earlier than I expected, and I pulled out some books I thought might help you. Though I hate to use them, some of the mythological encyclopedias are helpful as jumping-off points. I went over them during dinner, and I think I do have a lead for you, actually."

"Really?" Jenna asked, surprised. "That's great."

"I'm glad to be of help," Indira confessed, as she lifted a small pile of books onto the table. "I was feeling a bit useless with the police. Based partially on your suspicion of me, I believe, they're looking into some of the students that I've had, not to mention my teaching assistants. Which, though I hate to admit it, makes a great deal of sense. Some of them have also studied comparative mythology and theology. Of course, I'd vouch for my T.A.'s but how do you really know?"

Jenna could relate. There was a time when she almost believed that her half brother, Pierce, was a killer. It had made her feel nauseated.

"Have you told the police about the connection to the stone circle at the site today?" she asked.

"Not yet. I'm going to, of course. That's why I'm a consultant. But frankly, I don't know that they'll be able to make much of it, and I doubt you will, either. It's just another bit of information that doesn't seem to lead anywhere. On the other hand, you people see things in a different light, so maybe it will help you."

The teakettle whistled, and Indira fixed them each a cup. While she was doing so, she pointed at the largest book on the table in front of Jenna.

"That's where I found the first link. Since it was a stone circle, I thought to look into Celtic and Druidic mythology and ancient rituals. But there didn't seem to be any link to the other things found at the site, or that drawing Dr. Slikowski told me about."

She brought the tea over, and they both sipped carefully. Jenna was growing impatient, but she didn't want to be rude. After a few moments Indira set her tea aside and started flipping through the book.

"This isn't really my area, of course, and most people are blissfully unaware of things they don't feel they need to know. But suffice it to say, Celtic beliefs descended from the people of Gaul—"

"Which is ancient France, right?" Jenna said quickly.

Indira smiled. "Very good. Yes. In the section on the Celtic mythology of Gaul, I found this photograph."

The professor pointed to a small stone figure, turning the book around so Jenna wasn't looking at it upside down. When she got a good look, Jenna's eyes widened.

"That's him," she said.

For it was. The figure was an old man with a long white beard, whose tongue was pierced through and connected to his ears by two small chains.

"I guess a lot of people would be disappointed to know that piercing isn't quite as original and rebellious as they'd like to think," she added, smiling. Then she read aloud from the caption beneath the photo. " 'Stone carved figure representing Ogmios, god of eloquence, champion of the gods, and . . .' "

Jenna looked up at Indira. "Guide of the dead?"

"Exactly my thought," Indira replied. Then she picked two other books from the stack and handed them to Jenna. "I looked briefly at these. You should be able to find more about Ogmios in here, I think. Just please return them when you can."

"As soon as I'm done," Jenna promised. "Thanks so much."

Indira smiled, and soon the conversation turned to more mundane things, like classes and work and life in general. When her teacup was drained, Jenna asked Indira if she could look at the shelves of books in the other room, and the professor led the way. Most of the novels there, including several first editions, belonged to Indira's roommate, Carol, and Jenna didn't dare ask if she could borrow one. But it was nice to look. It seemed like fate when she ran across an original printing of Jack London's *The Sea Wolf,* one of her favorite novels.

Eventually, she realized that eight o'clock had come and gone. The party had started at eight, and she knew that Yoshiko and Hunter would give her a hard time if she was really late.

"Thanks again," she said as she stood on the front step, zipping up her jacket while trying to hold on to the books Indira had lent her. "I'll get these back to you soon."

"Take your time," the professor said kindly.

As soon as she shut the door, Jenna hurried down the street toward the T station. She'd have to stop at her room to drop off the books, and that was going to make her even later.

The streetlights flashing overhead, shining through the windshield, had started to lull Danny Mariano into a sort of trance, a numb, quiet place where he could shut his brain off for just a few minutes. And he needed those minutes, after the day he'd had. An old rap song started up on KISS 108, and though he really couldn't stand rap, Danny just let it play. It only served to increase the weird rhythm of the trance he was in.

A traffic light turned red up ahead, and he was forced to apply the brakes. He was only a couple of blocks from Somerset P.D. headquarters, and he was looking forward to going home right after he checked in with Audrey.

He'd hated his day. His week, actually, if he had to focus on it that much. Never mind the constant abuse he'd had to take from his lieutenant and fellow officers—Audrey mostly—about going on that little stakeout with Jenna last Saturday. That was bad enough. But today had topped it off like a rotting cherry.

Professor Arora had given the Cambridge P.D. a list of her students and teaching assistants from the past four years. She'd added to it a handful of other professors at area schools who didn't teach a course like hers—it was fairly unique—but who were likely to have some knowledge of the subject matter. It was a hell of a list, even after they'd split the thing up with the Cambridge cops. Flannery had been more than happy to have their help, and now Danny was sort of wishing they'd never offered.

But the day was over—that was something, at least.

They'd started with the phone, of course, crossing off people who no longer lived in the area, one guy who had died, and several who turned out to live locally but happened to be out of the country. Then the interview process began. Nearly everyone was willing to help once they'd dropped Professor Arora's name.

They weren't nearly as helpful in person, Danny had found—much to his regret. And to his current state of mind.

It was a lark to them, a bit of excitement in the otherwise dull day of the average college or graduate student or academic. He found them, for the most part, to fit squarely into one of two categories. Some were fascinated, as though they were watching a drama on television. Others were arrogant and dismissive.

None of them gave him a damn thing that advanced the investigation a single iota. Most of them, of course, had alibis for at least one of the three murders. Others, Danny decided—based upon Dr. Slikowski's autopsy reports and theories—were simply too tall to be the killer. His list had included more than thirty people, and only two of them, both former teaching assistants, seemed like real candidates to him.

Both were men.

He didn't dare suggest to Audrey that he wasn't looking hard at the two guys because Jenna thought the killer was a woman—he knew what that would look like to her, and he had to wonder if she wasn't right. But Slick hadn't discounted Jenna's theory, and Danny himself kept coming back to the taser. The fact that the killer was hitting the victims with high voltage first, to take them down quietly, didn't necessarily mean it was a woman. But somehow, it all just sounded right.

So he planned to follow up on the thin alibis the two guys had given him, but Danny didn't like either one of them as a murder suspect.

He was still grumbling a few minutes later when he walked up the stairs and into the homicide squad room. Audrey was behind her desk, keying something into her computer.

"Hey," he said.

"I was starting to worry about you," Audrey replied, offering a half smile.

Possibly, he thought, *as a peace offering.*

"Yeah. Smart people are long-winded," he complained.

"So are morons," Audrey reminded him. "They both like to hear themselves talk."

Danny managed a smile at that. "I hope you've got more than I do."

"I'm following up on a few candidates. Nothing jumped out at me, though. I talked to Flannery, too. He claims he's got a half-dozen solid suspects. I think he's blowing smoke." She leaned back in her chair and regarded him carefully. "You all right?"

Danny grimaced. "That supposed to be funny?"

"No."

He shrugged. "Then, no, I'm not all right. But it's nothing a beer and bad cable won't help fix. I have a couple of possibles, but I don't think much of their chances."

Audrey hit a few more keys and then shut her computer down. She stood up and grabbed her jacket. "I'm going home," she said. "We can go over our pool of suspects in the morning. I'd ask if that was all right with you, but I have a feeling you're halfway out the door already."

"Thanks," Danny said.

"Oh, before I forget, why don't you take that home with you," Audrey added, pointing to several pages on his desk. "It's the story related to that Japanese mythology thing, Izanagi. I faxed it over to Walter Slikowski also, so your girlfriend can do her girl-detective thing."

Danny turned to glare at her, real anger boiling up in him. Then he saw that Audrey was smiling. He was surprised. She'd made her feelings about Jenna, and Danny's flirtation with her, perfectly clear.

"Sorry," she said. "Couldn't help it. I like to kick a man when he's down. Go back to your place, do your homework, and then go to bed."

With a sigh, Danny nodded, his anger disappearing. He dropped all his files on his desk, pushed in the chair, and headed down the stairs. In the parking lot, he waved to Audrey as she drove off.

When he got home, he read about Izanagi. It was a chilling story from ancient Japanese mythology, about a god whose mate, Izanami, had died and gone to the netherworld, called Yomi. He went to get her back—sort of like Orpheus, Danny thought, surprising himself with this bit of knowledge that popped up out of nowhere—and was enraged to discover that her body had started to decay, squirming with maggots and snakes. Izanagi later blocked the entrance to the netherworld and never returned.

"He never died," Danny whispered to himself, sprawled across the bed with only one weak light to read by. "He never died," he repeated, almost tasting the words.

Slick had told Danny and Audrey about Jenna's suggestion that the killer might be so indiscriminate because he or she was dying and believed in this transmigration crap enough to try to make it happen. This story clearly fed into that theory.

"Audrey must have loved this," he muttered to himself. Then he flung the papers onto the floor and turned out the light.

Light bedtime reading, he thought. *Sure to inspire pleasant dreams.*

‾‾‾‾‾‾‾‾‾‾
‾‾‾‾‾‾‾‾‾‾
‾‾‾‾‾‾‾‾‾‾
‾‾‾‾‾‾‾‾‾‾
‾‾‾‾‾‾‾‾‾‾
‾‾‾‾‾‾‾‾‾‾

chapter 11

When Jenna arrived at the AOPi sorority house, the party was well underway. As long as things didn't get too loud, and nobody got hurt or made a public spectacle of themselves out on the street, the police would pretty much leave them alone. From what she'd heard, Somerset went through periods of almost Prohibition-level paranoia about partying. Other times, the school's administration stepped back and let the parties happen, within reason.

All in all, despite the keg and what the sorority called "AOPunch," things seemed relatively controlled. Bodies gyrated, some of them sweaty in spite of the open windows and the November air, but there were clumps of people standing around talking over the music, or in line for punch or beer. Jenna hadn't attended a fraternity party yet, but from what she'd heard, this was similar, only scaled down somewhat. And just from the first minute and a half at the party, she was pretty sure she didn't want to stay. It was a bit overwhelming.

"Jenna!"

She turned quickly, ducking her head to peer between a couple grinding to old TLC, and saw Caitlyn and Olivia waving her over. They were standing with a guy Jenna didn't recognize, all broad shoulders and buzz cut.

"Hey!" she said, raising her voice a bit because of the music. "This is nuts!" She glanced around to indicate that she meant the party.

"Isn't it great!" Caitlyn replied gleefully.

"Wow," Jenna said, not wanting to be rude.

Great might not have been my first choice.

"This is Brian Jansen," Olivia said, nodding toward buzz-cut guy. "He's the president of DTD." She said that part as though it was important, then turned to Brian. "This is our friend Jenna Blake. We're on the same floor at Sparrow."

Brian smiled, nodded approvingly. "Yeah, Caitlyn told me about you."

He said her name with a sort of proprietary tone, and Jenna wondered if Brian and Caitlyn were *together*. She supposed he was sort of handsome in that jock way, but he didn't really do anything for her.

"Yeah?" Jenna asked. "What'd she tell you?"

"You're the chick who works at the morgue, right?" he asked, still nodding, still smiling. "That's wild."

Jenna's smile became very frosty. "Yeah," she said. "Wild." Then she turned to the other girls. "Have you seen Yoshiko and Hunter?"

Olivia had her punch glass halfway to her lips, but she paused to nod. "Yeah," she said. "They were looking for you before. I think they're upstairs playing Trivia Buzz."

Not quite sure what the hell Olivia was talking about, Jenna excused herself and pushed her way through the partyers toward the large center staircase. There were a lot of people standing and sitting on the stairs as well, but she managed to step past or over them to get to the second floor. Just across from the top of the stairs was a double-size entryway that opened into a common area—what must have been a sitting room when the house had first been built in the 1800s. There were at least a dozen people in the room, crowded around a Trivial Pursuit board, and all of them had drinks.

Which sort of explains Trivia Buzz, she thought.

Hunter and Yoshiko sat together on the far side of the room, beneath the windows that looked out at the trees behind AOPi. Yoshiko rolled a die, and it came up four. As she was moving her game piece around the board, Hunter glanced up and spotted Jenna.

"Hey!" he said, grinning. "It's about time you showed up."

Suddenly, Jenna found herself smiling too. She had been uncomfortable since she had walked through the door, but now that she'd found her friends, and saw the game going on—a lot more private than the chaos downstairs—she started to relax.

"Come on, J, you're on our team," Yoshiko said.

There were quick introductions to the rest of the people around the board, a few of whom Jenna knew from one class or another. Hunter slipped a glass of punch into her hand, and when they settled down, one of the players, Kelly something, read a question from a card.

"What was Roman emperor Augustus's real name before he became Caesar?"

It took a moment for Jenna to recall that it had been Hunter and Yoshiko's turn when she came in, and that meant the question was directed at their team.

"I know this!" Hunter said in exasperation.

Yoshiko rolled her eyes. "That means he thinks he knew it once, but doesn't have a clue," she said to the other players.

Jenna looked at her roommate, frowning as she tried to remember the answer. "I know this," she said, a bit apologetically. "Really."

"I hope you do, 'cause I don't remember," Yoshiko admitted.

Then, suddenly, Jenna had it. "Octavian!"

Kelly-something grumbled and put the card back into the box. She and Kyle, the guy she was teamed with, both took a drink of their punch, then passed the box along. Jenna realized that the game had a double jeopardy thing going, then. If you got a question wrong, you had to take a drink. And if you asked a question and the other team got it right—drink.

None of the three of them had the answer to the next question, something about a world record at the Indianapolis 500.

The punch was good. Not too strong. Then it was someone else's turn.

"So what was your big errand?" Yoshiko asked. "Where'd you go?"

Jenna didn't want to get into it, so she just smiled a bit. "I was having tea," she said, and left it at that.

The game went on for almost an hour before Jenna decided she had to hit the bathroom. Yoshiko told her where to find it, and Jenna stepped over Hunter and around the others and went downstairs. As she was making her way back to the game, though, she pushed between two groups of people and came face-to-face with Damon's friend Brick.

"Hey, Jenna!" he said happily. "How you doing?"

"Hi, Brick. I'm good. But I think I've had too much punch."

"Maybe you should drink beer instead," he suggested. "Where are you hanging out?"

"We're playing Trivia Buzz upstairs," she said. "Come up if you get bored sweeping the party for girls to impress."

"I'll do that," he replied, laughing, eyes alive with humor and self-awareness. "But you know, there are a lot of girls here."

Jenna laughed as well and shook her head. She liked Brick because he was ultraconfident, but with his personality, it never really seemed like arrogance.

"Talk to you later," she said, and started off again.

Then Brick put a hand on her shoulder. "Hey, hold up a second."

Jenna turned and looked at him curiously. Brick's smile had become conspiratorial and mischievous. His eyes lit up as he glanced around the room, his demeanor making it clear he intended to share a secret. Barely realizing she was doing it, Jenna leaned forward a bit.

"I shouldn't tell you this, but I'm gonna," he said.

His eyes locked on hers, intimate, but neither romantic nor threatening in any way. They saw each other clearly then, and it occurred to Jenna how infrequently people looked one another in the eye and really connected. He had something to share.

"Hunter was telling us about you asking that cop out," Brick said in a low voice.

Jenna blushed, angry at Hunter, but only a little.

"Gotta tell you, girl, my boy was a little jealous," Brick told her. "He gave with the 'just friends' thing, but I think somewhere in his head there's more going on than that."

Jenna blinked in surprise. "You mean Damon?" she asked, though she knew full well who Brick meant.

He laughed and looked away, dismissing the question. Then he leaned forward and kissed her on the cheek, and then he was gone into the crowd, already starting to move with the music, dancing, getting the attention that he always did, at a party or onstage. Brick was what romance novelists called a rogue. Jenna thought the word fit him very well.

Damon, she thought, more confused than ever.

Then, almost as if the thought had summoned him,

he was there in front of her. When he spotted her, he smiled broadly.

"Hey," he said. "I didn't know you were going to be here."

"Yoshiko and Hunter are upstairs," she informed him. "We were playing Trivia Buzz. I'm headed back up there now."

"Oh." Damon nodded, but he seemed a little disappointed. Jenna noticed a couple of girls moving by, and how they gazed at him. One of them very obviously checked out his butt. Jenna smiled at Damon, and wondered if he recognized the attention he got.

"It isn't really fair, though, the three of us on one team," she said quickly. "I could use a partner."

He grinned broadly. "You're on."

They linked arms going up the stairs. On the way up, they passed Olivia, who was talking to another girl. Jenna said hello, and Olivia greeted them both, but there was a kind of scowl on her face that made Jenna stiffen.

At the top of the stairs, Damon turned to her, smiling and frowning at the same time. "Let it go," he said.

And she did.

She and Damon returned to the game as a brand-new team. They laughed a lot, drank too much punch, and missed some easy questions.

It was nice. Very nice.

Wednesday morning, Jenna was woken once again by the phone ringing. For a moment she thought to ask

Yoshiko to get it, but she was already awake, and dragged herself out of bed.

"We've got to turn that ringer off at night," Yoshiko grumbled from her bunk.

"Hello?" Jenna rasped.

"Hi, honey."

"Mom. It's early."

"Sorry. I'm on my way to the hospital. I have an early surgery today, and I know you have class in a little while."

"No problem, what's up?"

"We need to talk about your job," April said bluntly.

"Again?"

"Jenna, I saw you on the eleven o'clock news last night. At that murder in Cambridge. With Walter Slikowski." Her mother's voice sounded distant and tinny, almost robotic. "I barely slept last night. I know you're almost nineteen, you're an adult. Fine. But I'm your mother, and that means I never stop telling you what I think, no matter how much you wish I would."

"I never asked you to stop," Jenna said. "But I have to make my own decisions."

"Fine," April said, sounding snippy now. "But here's my two cents. You've nearly been killed on this job a couple of times. Now you're at murder scenes, on the news, hanging out with the cops. And all of that when you should be at school. I'm not even going to ask what time that was, and whether you should have been in class."

Jenna flushed, feeling a little guilty because her

mother was right about that, at least. She had skipped class yesterday morning. But she wasn't going to let that cloud the main issue.

"Mom, you're a surgeon. You've seen your share of cops, never mind murders. How many patients have you lost? I've had my arms elbow deep in dead men, and that's the job. You wanted me in medicine—well, this is probably the closest I'll get."

"That isn't what this is about, Jenna," her mother argued. "And, yeah, I've seen all those things, but you're just too close, honey, don't you see it? Nobody ever tried to kill me for attempting to save someone's life."

Jenna sighed, reached up to massage her temple, and then just gave up. "Know what, Mom? I have a class to get to. You have surgery this morning. Can we just talk about this when I come home for Thanksgiving?"

For a moment her mother didn't say anything at all. Then Jenna heard her take a long breath.

"Fine," April said. "But please be careful, honey. I just love you."

"I love you, too."

During her classes that day, Jenna went over her conversation with her mother. She found that she had no intention whatsoever of leaving her job, and that amazed her. A few months earlier, she would never have imagined that she would be involved in anything like pathology, or forensics, or murder investigations.

Now she felt as though she'd found her footing, found the path that she was supposed to follow.

Somehow, she'd have to make her mother understand that.

After her last class, she headed over to work. Dyson and Slick were down in autopsy, so she left her jacket and took the elevator to the basement. When she walked in, the two doctors greeted her, but their joint demeanor was very grave. They were in the midst of examining the chest cavity and organs of a boy, no more than eight, whose entire body seemed to have been crushed like an empty soda can.

Jenna cringed at the sight, felt a surge of horror at the boy's fate, and at being so close to him. But then she took a deep breath of the formaldehyde-laden air of the autopsy room, and started slipping into her gown and gloves.

"You always choose the best days to come to work," Dyson said grimly from behind his mask.

"Don't I, though?"

Dyson and Slick had both made a habit of suggesting that she sit out the worst of the autopsies they performed. Sometime in the past week or so, they'd stopped doing that. It felt like she'd somehow graduated to some new level. Now a part of her wished she could go back.

But she wanted to know how the boy died, and if someone was responsible for his death. She wanted to be certain that she was a part of the team that brought that to light.

"What happened to him?" she asked.

"He was run over by a truck," Slick replied, and she could hear the anger and sadness in his voice. "But I don't think that's what killed him."

Jenna looked at him in confusion.

Dyson nodded. "Contusions all over his head and neck and chest that didn't come from the truck, not to mention a serious blunt-object cranial trauma that also didn't come from the truck."

"So someone left him in the road to cover up the fact that he was murdered?"

Slick stopped his work removing the intestines to look at Jenna. With the mask hiding the rest of his face, his eyes looked very serious behind his wire-rimmed spectacles. "The driver stopped the truck. The boy's father came running out, screaming at him, claiming that his son had been running across the road and stumbled. He fell down in front of the truck."

Jenna felt sick as she looked down at the boy.

His father did this, she thought. But with the nausea incited by that thought came another. *And because of Slick and Dyson, because of what we do, the bastard's going to pay.*

She'd never give up this job. Her path, through college and medical school, had never seemed clearer to her than it did at that moment. Calmly, she moved in next to Dyson and helped him weigh and dissect and label organ samples. They did much of the work in silence. It wasn't until they were nearly done that they began to speak again.

"So, Jenna, it looks like your instincts were on target again," Dyson said.

"How do you mean?"

Slick went to the low stainless steel sink that had been installed just so he could reach it from his chair. He ripped off his gloves and threw them in the hazardous waste bin, then scrubbed his hands under the water.

"I had a fax from Audrey Gaines last night," the M.E. explained. "I also had a conversation with her this morning. Apparently the Japanese mythology connected to the second murder has to do with a god who found a way to keep himself from dying."

Jenna's eyes widened. "Seriously?"

"Very much so," Slick replied, and finally managed a small smile. "In fact, both Audrey and Danny think that this might be the break they need to narrow their suspects down. And Audrey said Danny wouldn't have recognized it at all if I hadn't told him about your theory to that effect."

Jenna beamed. It wasn't the end, not by a long shot. But she felt that, in some small way, she had begun to make up for the embarrassment of the whole situation with Indira Arora. Which reminded her . . .

"Oh, by the way," she said. "Professor Arora lent me a couple of books that relate to that stone circle at the third site. Apparently it has to do with the worship of a god who was supposed to guide the dead to the afterworld."

"Which all feeds into the main theory on the killer,"

Dyson observed. "Man, this woman really is desperate. What's next, Scientology?"

Jenna was about to give him a hard time for joking about it, but then she saw that his expression was sincere. He was just as much at a loss as everyone else.

"The killer must truly believe that this is possible," Dr. Slikowski said grimly. "If that's true, there's no telling what he or she will try next."

"I have an even scarier thought," Jenna admitted. "What if she's right? What if it *is* possible?"

They both stared at her as though she'd lost her mind. "What?" she asked. "Don't tell me neither of you has thought of it. Especially you, Dr. Slikowski. You were there when Indira told us that story. I mean, I'm not saying I believe it, but, okay, *what if?*"

Neither of them had a quick response to that one.

In the homicide division offices of the Cambridge police department, Danny and Audrey sat in an interview room with Joe Flannery, going over the files of information they'd collected about the fifteen people from their original list that they considered possible suspects. Of the fifteen, six were women. Danny wasn't about to argue that they should look at just the women—that wouldn't have made sense anyway, in case that part of it was wrong—but he was going to focus on them and let Audrey and Flannery pay more attention to the men.

Now it was just a matter of trying to find out if any of them had any serious health problems. Since there was a patient-doctor privacy standard, that meant they would need to either confront the suspects directly or ask their acquaintances if they'd been ill. Unless the doctors would talk, of course.

"Y'know," Danny said in exasperation, "sometimes I think it would be much easier if we could just hack into the medical files."

"Wouldn't it, though?" Audrey replied. "Problem with that is, it's a crime."

"Yeah," Flannery added. "I'd have to lock you up, Mariano."

Danny grumbled in frustration. *But,* he told himself, *at least we have somewhere to start.* And in reality it shouldn't really take that long to find out if any of the people on their list had a terminal illness. On the other hand . . .

"It just seems like such a slim lead, y'know?" he said. "I mean, this is all we've got."

"Yeah," Flannery agreed. "For the moment, it *is.* So can we get down to it now? Before it happens again?"

Danny picked up a stack of files and started leafing through them.

She was coughing. It made her feel weak. In turn, feeling weak and sick and so damned tired made her furious.

Her grip tightened on the taser.

Again, that tickle in her throat, threatening a cough that might bring up blood. But she couldn't allow the cough; she had to stifle it. She didn't dare give herself away.

Not now. Not when she could see the girl walking down the path toward her, slender and pretty, perfect. The moonlight was enough to see by, despite the sparse clouds above.

This would be it.

This *had* to be it.

She had arranged everything on the grass between a copse of trees and the wrought iron fence. There was a risk here, so close to the dormitories, but she had chosen the least traversed area of the Harvard campus.

The cough was coming again, and there was nothing she could do to stop it.

"Damn," she whispered to herself, watching the girl approach, so close.

Then she realized that it was propitious. It was perfect, if she could time it just right. She stepped out from between a couple of trees, and let the cough come, hard and ragged, tearing up her throat like ground glass.

"Are you all right?" came the girl's voice, high and with the faintest hint of Britain.

She let the cough come again, wracking her body.

The girl came up beside her, touched her arm, wanting to help.

When the coughing subsided, she brought up the taser.

chapter 12

The heater in Danny's car rattled and blew out a weak stream of barely warm air. The sky was clear blue, not a cloud in sight; the sun gleamed off the windshield, revealing with its intensity exactly how dirty the car was. Despite the sun, however, it was cold outside, barely forty on the Somerset Savings Bank clock that he glanced at as he drove past it. And with the wind, it felt colder.

It was too early in the year for it to feel that cold.

But there was something very right about it, as well, at least as far as Danny was concerned.

All during the drive from Somerset to Cambridge, along Massachusetts Avenue to Harvard University, Danny and Audrey barely spoke. For his own part, Danny could think of nothing to say. With this latest murder, the stakes were raised, somehow. One more body, that was all. And yet Danny couldn't help but think of it as killer: four; cops: zero. Despite their suspicions and the work they'd been doing interviewing potential suspects, they were no closer to having a damn clue as to who was behind these killings than they had been after the first one.

Four dead. And the promise of more if they didn't catch a break.

But we're not that goddamn lucky.

They'd finally called in the FBI profiling unit, and pretty soon, the media attention might force the mayors of the two cities to ask for more direct involvement from the FBI. Danny hated to admit it, even to himself, but he was starting to wonder if that might not be a good idea. Someone new might be able to look at the thing from a completely different perspective.

"You're quiet," Audrey said, as the car glided through the mass of edgy humanity that thronged Harvard Square.

Danny raised an eyebrow. "So are you."

"I'm always like this. It's called being a cranky bitch," she replied, and managed a half smile.

Surprised by her candor, particularly since things had been a bit tense between them lately, Danny attempted to return the smile, but the result didn't quite accomplish it.

"Just starting to feel like I'm on the losing team, I guess," he confessed.

"I know the feeling," Audrey replied. Then, after glancing around at the people in the square for a moment, she looked back at Danny. "If your girlfriend's there, I'll try to be nicer."

Danny braked to avoid hitting a car that had stopped short in front of him, and gave Audrey a hard look. He didn't have to explain that Jenna wasn't his girlfriend. Audrey knew that. They'd talked about it enough. He was getting very tired of her attitude.

"Yeah," he grunted. "You do that. If you think you're capable."

"I'll manage," she said, again with a half smile.

She was trying to make up, or something. Danny wasn't sure he wanted to.

"Hey," Audrey said. "Maybe I should've minded my own business. I know I'm not your mother or your wife—which just tells me God still has a little love in his heart for me—but I figured being your partner and your friend meant I ought to speak my mind."

With a slow nod, Danny turned into one of the guest parking lots at Harvard University, not far from the fenced-in area where the murder had taken place. He remained silent as he pulled the car into a spot, and the two of them got out. Danny shivered a little against the cold and stuffed his hands into the deep pockets of his long wool coat. He had a suit on today, trying to be conscientious about the image people had of the department. The lieutenant had warned them this case would mean they'd be on the local news a lot, and he thought it would be helpful to community relations if they looked good.

"Great," Danny had mumbled to Audrey. "Now we're SPD's poster children."

Audrey had said nothing. But today, she wore a neatly pressed dark-green pantsuit that he'd never seen on her before. It didn't look much like her usual work outfits.

Outside the car Danny regarded her evenly, even a bit coldly. "Being my partner and my friend means you get to speak your mind," he echoed. "Yep. But that means once. As advice, not condemnation. And then you shut the hell up and let me make my own mistakes."

His tone clearly angered Audrey, and she lifted her chin slightly. "Yeah, you did that real well, Danny."

He sighed. "Look, I like Jenna. She's sharp and funny, and she's got a lot of personality. But that's as far as it goes. And I shouldn't have to explain myself to you."

Without waiting for a response, he spun on his heel and walked across the lot, between police and other crime scene vehicles. Audrey followed slowly after him. There were a couple of dozen people, mostly uniformed cops, milling around the area bordered with yellow police line tape, and most of them were shivering. Danny spotted a crime scene photographer, and some forensics guys, but he didn't know most of them because they were the Cambridge team. Still, it was a familiar enough scene.

Neither he nor Audrey had called Dr. Slikowski in their rush to get out to the site, but they'd assumed that Joe Flannery would have done so. Danny was a bit surprised not to see Slick's van. He was also surprised, since this was her campus, that Professor Arora was not with the representatives of the school administration.

A moment later Danny spotted Flannery and headed directly for him. Flannery was giving instructions to a couple of uniforms, but waved the men away as he saw Danny and Audrey approaching.

"Thanks for calling," Danny said as he walked up.

"Yeah, well, maybe I won't have to much longer," Flannery grumbled. "That little girl mighta been right. Our guy seems to like my town the best. Just my freakin' luck."

"What've we got?" Danny asked, peering past the burly cop at the tangle of humanity that surrounded the murder scene.

Flannery's eyes flickered over to Audrey and back to Danny. "Have a look."

They walked over together. Danny stopped at the edge of the yellow tape to glance around at the layout. It was clear the killer had lain in wait behind some shrubs and then dragged the victim back there to do the actual murder. But this was a college campus. Even in the wee hours of the morning, he figured there had to be *some* foot traffic.

"Witnesses?" he asked.

Flannery nodded. "Looks like we may have gotten lucky, finally. Got a guy says he saw something from his window, up there." Flannery pointed at a nearby dorm. It was far enough away that the killer could have reasonably expected not to be seen, particularly if she stayed behind the bushes most of the time, and if there weren't many lights on inside the rooms.

"Apparently he saw someone coming out of there about one-thirty this morning. He figured she was either with someone or doing something illegal, maybe throwing up from drinking too much. That was until he saw us all out here this morning."

Danny was still studying the window. Then it struck him, what Flannery had said. He turned and stared at the cop.

"She?"

"Yeah," Flannery shrugged, reluctant. "Looks like the girl was right. Witness described the suspect as five three or so, long dark hair, pulled back, in dark clothes, maybe sweats. Didn't get a good look at her face, though. From the description, it could even be that Blake kid."

Flannery was just being obnoxious with that, Danny knew. Nevertheless, he rolled his eyes.

"Danny."

He turned to see Audrey beckoning to him from beside the black shroud–covered corpse that lay on the ground twenty feet away. Audrey had pulled the dark sheet back, and Danny got a good look at the dead girl's face. She had the dark eye drawn in marker on her forehead, and she'd been strangled, but there didn't seem to have been any other damage, not like the last two murders.

"I don't get it," he said to his partner. "Doesn't the violence usually escalate in a case like this?"

Audrey nodded. "Maybe she's getting tired. Maybe we're on the right track with this illness thing. Or maybe someone came along and she figured it was time to go."

Danny had noticed the small iron bowl near the dead woman's head, and hadn't thought a whole lot about it. Something to look into, sure, but it didn't seem all that remarkable to him. Now, though, he saw that she clutched something in her hand, and he bent closer to have a look at it.

His eyes widened. "Is this—"

"Yes," Audrey replied grimly.

"Yes, what?" Flannery asked gruffly, coming up behind them. He bent over the corpse and looked at what was clutched in the dead woman's hand. "I had 'em leave it all like this until you two could have a look. I was about to tell them to start picking up the evidence and getting the body over to SMU."

Danny took a moment to appreciate what Flannery had said. The Cambridge cop was being extremely cooperative, all things considered. Not every detective working on a shared jurisdiction case would have been so courteous. Flannery could be a real son of a bitch, but he was a pretty good cop, when it came down to it. Some cops might even have sent the corpse somewhere else to be autopsied, somewhere closer, but the Cambridge P.D. had asked for Dr. Slikowski's help on the case, so the DOA went to SMC.

"So? You gonna share?" Flannery prodded.

"Santeria," Audrey said.

Flannery turned to her and frowned. Danny stood up and faced them both, straightening his tie.

"Like voodoo?" Flannery asked.

"Not really," Audrey said, shaking her head. "Santeria is a religion that comes down from some of the tribes of the Congo. There are elements that might remind you of voodoo, but it isn't really that similar. Ninety percent of Santeria is white magic. Spells and potions and charms, that sort of thing."

Flannery glanced down at the dead woman, at the thing in her hand. "But not all."

"No," Audrey replied. "Not all. Some of the people who practice Santeria become *brujerias*. They invite possession by malicious spirits of the dead. The pot there, that's probably a *nganga*. It would contain the power of a *brujeria*. The bone in her hand is a magical scepter."

"It's a bone wrapped in a black scrap of somebody's sweatshirt or something," Flannery said doubtfully.

"It's a scepter, in Santeria," Audrey explained. "It should be a human tibia bone." She looked around, frowning. "Was there a candle?"

Flannery blinked. "Actually, there was. We found it with a broken dish, little white saucer, in the bush over there. Didn't know if it was related."

"It is," Audrey said confidently, frowning. "The killer must have tossed it there before she left."

Danny had a picture in his head of the woman, frustrated that once again she had failed in her desire to take up residence in someone else's body, tossing the candle and dish to one side. He only wished that he had a face to put in the picture, an identity for the killer.

"How do you know all this crap?" Flannery asked Audrey. "You got relatives back in the Congo or something?"

Audrey lowered her chin slightly, glaring dangerously up at Flannery, her eyes nearly hidden in shadows. Danny stepped between them before she could take a swing at the other cop, but that didn't mean that he wasn't thinking about doing exactly the same thing.

"We had a case a couple years ago," Danny explained. "Guy trying to become a *brujeria* killed his sister when she tried to stop him. The ritual was a lot like this—without the Hindu elements we've seen throughout. My guess is our perp was trying to do the ritual *for* the DOA. Maybe hoping it would pull her spirit into the dead woman's body."

Flannery shook his head. "All this stuff is nuts," he said in exasperation, and threw up his hands.

When he walked away, Danny followed him, leaving Audrey to glare at Flannery's back and to contemplate the murder scene a little more. When they were far enough away from Audrey, Danny cast a sidelong glance at Flannery.

"You a bigot, Joe, or are you just ignorant?" he muttered.

"What'd you say?" Flannery challenged, rounding on him, fists clenched.

"That comment to Audrey, about the Congo," Danny elaborated, though he was sure Flannery knew exactly what he was talking about. "I was just thinking what a nice little bit of cooperation we have going on here, and then you have to go and say something as stupid as that. What the hell's in your head?"

Flannery cast a quick glance at Audrey, then looked back uncertainly at Danny.

"Hell, kid, I didn't mean anything by it," the older detective said. "She knew her stuff. It's just what popped into my head is all."

Danny nodded, rolling his eyes. "Yeah. Before thinking maybe she got that information from an education, or maybe on the job, you automatically figured, she's black, so she probably has relatives in Africa. But you didn't mean anything by it. Which would mean the answer to my question would be 'ignorant,' I guess."

Sobered, but still angered by Danny's tone, Flannery puffed himself up a bit. "You want me to apologize to her. That it?"

"I want you to realize I just saved you from having her make you bleed," Danny said grimly. "And I only did it to save me and Audrey the paperwork."

With that, he turned and walked back toward the dead woman. When he reached Audrey, he muttered, "Let's go," and kept moving. They got into the car together, and Danny drove them back toward Somerset.

"I don't need you taking up for me, Dan," Audrey said sternly, once they'd pulled out into traffic. "I don't appreciate it."

"We don't need that kind of trouble right now," he

told her. "But I wasn't about to let him walk away without making him realize he'd misspoken."

After a moment of silence, his partner looked at him again. "So what did you say?" she asked.

"I put the fear of Audrey in him."

They both grinned at that.

After her American lit class, Jenna met her father for lunch at the Campus Center. He'd called that morning, sounding very stressed, and asked her to meet him. Now she was dreading it. They'd never been close, at least not until recently, but Jenna knew that if Frank had been stressed about his book or about his growing relationship with Shayna, he would have sounded terse and distant.

But that morning, he'd been very focused.

When she walked up to find him waiting for her at the entrance to the Asian-motifed building, she was surprised to see him smiling.

"Hey," she said, trying to sound upbeat. She stood on her toes and kissed his bearded cheek.

"You look great," Frank said as they walked into the Campus Center. "Everything's going well?"

"Yeah," she replied, sort of noncommittally. "I mean, I think I'm doing pretty well this semester. I think I'm on track for a 3.6 or higher."

They were in line with their trays. Frank looked at her with obvious surprise. "That's great, honey," he said. "With all you've had to deal with, you should be extra proud that you've been able to do so well."

"Thanks," Jenna said, happy in spite of her anxiety. "So what about you? How're things with Shayna?"

Frank smiled again. "Going really well. Kind of scary, actually," he confessed. "I keep expecting her to reveal her true self, y'know, the nagging witch beneath the surface? But so far, so good."

A thought flashed across Jenna's mind. *Is that what he thinks of Mom?* But she pushed it away. Her father and mother had been divorced a long time, and there was no real love lost between them now. Whatever they thought of each other really didn't matter.

"Any romance in *your* life, Jenna?"

"Huh?" She blushed a bit. "Well, now that you mention it, there is a guy I think I like."

"You think?"

"Well, I mean, I like him. But I don't know if anything's going to come of it."

Her father smiled. "Keep me posted. You know I'll want to meet him."

Jenna rolled her eyes. "That's all I need—Daddy passing judgment on my dates." She sighed. "But you'll be the first to know if I have a boyfriend, all right?"

They slid their trays onto a table amidst the babble of students and teachers and visitors. It was early for lunch, but the place was already very busy. Jenna had grabbed a grilled-chicken caesar salad, and her father had the courage to order a burrito, the very idea of which frightened Jenna. The Campus Center might have been a step above the dining halls, but it was still college food.

"So," Jenna said, as her father took a bite of burrito. "You wanted to meet me today so you could tell me how worried you are about me and my job."

He looked a bit surprised that she'd brought it up, and chewed quickly, preparing to reply. Jenna didn't give him a chance.

"Mom already talked to me about it. I'll tell you the same thing I told her. I like the job. I'm doing fine in all my classes. I don't have any intention of quitting." When she was through speaking, she nodded firmly as though that settled it.

Frank didn't see it that way. "I know what you're going to say, Jenna. I set you up with this interview. I suggested this as a possible career path. Well, I'm glad you see it as a career you'd like to pursue. But the whole point of the future is that it is not *now*. I never imagined, when I called Walter Slikowski to see if he'd meet with you, that he'd have you out at murder sites and such. I thought you'd be in the hospital all the time. And even that can be dangerous."

Jenna frowned and looked more closely at her father. "You want me to quit?"

"Yes," he told her. "I think you should quit. Absolutely, I do. Take your time with your life, Jenna. You're growing up too fast, and I'm not just saying that because I'm your father. You should be enjoying the freedoms and challenges of college life—"

"I am!" she snapped. "Didn't you hear any of what I was saying before?"

"Yes, of course, but—"

"But nothing," Jenna said flatly. "You want me to quit. Message received. Now here's the reply. *No.* Slick doesn't have me out at murder sites, he's not pushing me to do anything like that. *I'm* pushing. It's what I want. It *means* something, Dad, and *that* means something to me. So, I'm sorry, but *no.*"

Frank seemed angry, but he didn't reply, only nodded slowly. His jaw was set, and he set about eating his lunch. After a moment Jenna did the same. It was nearly five minutes before either of them spoke again.

"I only want what's best for you," he said meekly.

Jenna stared at him. "I'm eighteen years old, Dad. Maybe I'll make mistakes along the way, but I will decide what's best for me."

The rest of lunch was awkward, but by the time they went their separate ways, father and daughter seemed to have reconciled. After her European history class, though, Jenna didn't go back to her dorm. Instead, she headed over to the medical center. She wanted to know if there had been any developments, and she didn't feel like waiting until the following afternoon, when she was next scheduled to work.

Arriving at the medical examiner's office, Jenna discovered that Slick and Dyson were in the midst of an autopsy and went downstairs to join them. When she walked into the autopsy room, neither of the doctors seemed the least bit surprised to see her.

"Good afternoon, Jenna," Slick said amiably.

She saw the black marker on the dead woman's forehead, and her heart sank. "Another one?" she asked, but it wasn't really a question, and neither of them saw fit to answer it.

"Did you learn anything from the books that Professor Arora loaned us?" Slick asked as he worked.

Someone's a bit tense, she thought, watching him. Then she realized that they were all a bit tense, and she wondered if it was due to the latest murder. It wasn't just that the woman had been killed that distressed them. It was that the killings now seemed to have become so regular. Each time a life was taken, the next one seemed more inevitable.

"Nothing that seemed all that significant," she admitted gravely. "Just our psycho's latest shot at immortality. Pretty much what we knew before."

Slick appeared distracted by her tone. He looked thoughtful for a moment as he studied her.

"You were right, by the way," he said. "There was a witness. The killer is a woman."

Jenna gave a sort of halfhearted chuckle. She knew she ought to feel some kind of triumph, but she felt nothing of the sort. If the witness had gotten a good look at the killer, she knew that would have been the first thing Slick told her when she walked in.

So they were still at square one.

Dyson cleared his throat a bit. "Y'know," he said, "as often as I see what I'd call insanity, it still stuns me. I mean, how could anyone believe that you could trade bodies with someone else, move your soul in like you're moving apartments? And even worse, how could you keep believing it after you'd tried it three or four times and it didn't work?"

"Madness," Slick agreed. "But remember, we have also posited that she is dying. Fear may give her the motivation to believe anything that's convenient."

Jenna shrugged. "Or maybe it isn't madness. Who are we to say? I mean, who knows? Remember that story Professor Arora told us? Maybe the killer thinks it's possible because she's done it before."

The doctors stared at her as though *she* was the crazy one.

Jenna sighed. "I have to go study Spanish. Call me if you hear anything."

chapter 13

J enna spent the balance of Thursday afternoon studying Spanish verb conjugations and then reading an assignment for her biology class, only half of which she understood. She had a reading assignment for history, as well, but she usually saved those and her readings for English for later at night. It was harder to focus on bio, so she tried to deal with that when she was wide awake.

It was nice and quiet on the floor that time of day, or at least relatively so. Jenna's phone didn't ring once, and she had the radio on Magic 106, with the volume on low. The soft rock station was almost too soothing, but at least it wasn't as distracting as something more upbeat would have been.

Around five o'clock, she found her eyes drooping a bit and put her biology text down. She lay on her bunk and allowed her eyes to close. *Just a few minutes,* she promised herself. *A short nap, and then dinner.* But just as she had started to really drift off, she heard the rattle of Yoshiko's key in the door, and her eyes popped open again. As her roommate entered, Jenna stretched languorously on the bed.

"Hey," she said, greeting Yoshiko.

"Well," Yoshiko replied in mock consternation, "I see you've had a productive afternoon."

Jenna smiled. "Yup."

"I don't feel like dining hall food tonight," Yoshiko said, pulling off her jacket. "I'm thinking Chinese."

Jenna grinned. "I thought you were *Japanese.*"

Yoshiko tossed her jacket onto Jenna's head with an amused scowl. "Fine," she said. "Make jokes. I thought, you know, hang out, maybe see if Hunter wants to join us, but, no, you've got to be a comedian."

"Yup," Jenna said again, using the same bored inflection as before. Slowly she dragged Yoshiko's jacket from her head. "Do you think we can ask Damon, too?"

With a slightly guilty look, Yoshiko shrugged. "I sort of already did."

Jenna's mouth dropped open. "You're unbelievable!" she said, laughing. "You've just got to get up in everybody's business."

Yoshiko raised one eyebrow. "I can always tell him we're not going," she offered.

"No, no," Jenna replied quickly. "That's all right. Just let me do the inviting from now on."

"As if you'd ever get around to it."

"I might," Jenna argued. "I'm just not sure what direction I want this to go."

"How about toward Panda Garden?" Yoshiko suggested. "The Szechuan's really spicy there."

Jenna glared at her, but couldn't keep a straight face. "What time are we going?" she asked.

"We were thinking about going to the movies after," Yoshiko said. "So probably not until seven or so. If you're not going to be starving by then."

"I'll have a yogurt or something," Jenna said, rolling the plan over in her mind. "Actually, do you think I could just meet you guys there?"

"I guess," Yoshiko replied, frowning. "What's up?"

"Nothing," Jenna assured her. "I just wanted to return the books I got from Professor Arora. If we're going to eat at Panda Garden, I might as well go all the way to Porter Square and then meet you guys at the restaurant on the way back."

"Okay," Yoshiko agreed. "Unless you want us to come with."

"Nah, it won't take long. Plus you can spend some time looking at the menu, figuring out just how spicy you want things to get."

Yoshiko laughed. "I thought that was the question you were supposed to be wrestling with."

"Wrestling," Jenna said thoughtfully. "*There's* an option."

Yoshiko grinned, scandalized. But in a good way.

"So now we sit and wait?" Danny asked.

He was leaning against the wall in the break room, sipping black coffee and feeling pretty useless. Audrey raised her eyebrows noncommittally, then walked over to shut off the TV that was bolted up high on the wall.

All of the six o'clock local newscasts had carried the story of the previous night's murder on the Harvard campus. They'd also reported the basic description of the suspect, as well as the estimated time of death, as provided by Dr. Slikowski. A contact number for the Cambridge P.D. had been flashed on the screen, with the request that anyone with information pertaining to the crime should contact the Cambridge authorities immediately.

It was very little to work with, Danny knew. But it was all they had. Audrey hadn't even dignified his question with an answer, and Danny understood. It had been a stupid question. A lot of detective work was sitting and waiting. It pissed him off.

"Maybe we'll get lucky," Audrey suggested. "Even at Harvard, there aren't *that* many people wandering around that time of night. Somebody had to have seen something, and with the time of death established by Slick and corroborated by our witness . . . maybe it won't *all* be crank calls."

That was the kicker, Danny knew. The Cambridge P.D. had provided a contact number. That was an engraved invite to hundreds of wackjobs to phone in confessions and accusations about aliens in government. But Audrey was right. It wasn't much, but it might be enough to get a solid lead.

One solid lead, he thought. *Just one.*

*　　*　　*

Though the bizarre murders of the past couple of weeks remained unsolved, and her frustration with that yet lingered, Jenna found herself feeling better than she had in quite some time. In some ways, she realized, she was actually in a better place in her life than she had been since she'd graduated from high school.

Despite the growing conflict with her parents over her job, the job itself was going very well. Even the dismissive attitudes of some of the cops she dealt with couldn't take that away from her. Slick wanted her around, even if she had sort of embarrassed him with the whole incident with Danny, when they'd shadowed Professor Arora. Even that couldn't taint what her job meant to her. It gave her a sense of self-worth that nothing else had ever come even remotely close to matching.

That was all external, though. Fortunately, she'd also found a new kind of contentment with her internal life, her emotions and thoughts and anxieties. In the wake of Melody's murder, she'd felt cast adrift in so many ways, but now that she had solidified things with Yoshiko and Hunter, she didn't feel quite so lonely anymore. The crush she had on Danny Mariano had become slightly awkward, but they were dealing. And in the meantime, she was starting to think something was brewing with Damon.

It was difficult for Jenna to even remember how depressed she'd been only days ago. But she did remember that it felt awful, and she didn't want to go back into that dark place anytime soon.

No. Things are good. I'm going to make sure they stay that way. *It's all in the attitude,* she told herself. *Appreciate what you've got.*

"You were a pitiful thing," she mumbled appreciatively to herself, as she waited on the platform for a T train to pull up.

That was over, though. Things were good now.

On the short train ride to Porter Square station, Jenna paid no attention to the people crunched in around her. This time of night, it was mostly Somerset students and couples headed out to Harvard Square or Boston for dinner or a concert or something. Maybe just to walk around. Boston was a great city for walking . . . and for shopping, as she would have been swift to remind her mother.

Gotta plan another shopping trip, she reminded herself.

A lot of the passengers were avant-garde, and of those, everyone seemed to be pierced somewhere unusual. The sweet aroma of incense filled the car she sat in, and she tried to pinpoint it by checking out a guy in a dashiki, only to realize it was coming from the goth-looking girl three seats down from him.

That was the Boston area. It might just as likely have been coming from one of the corporate types in dark suits. *Takes all kinds around here,* she thought. Then it occurred to her how unusual the train ride was. Boston certainly had its share of tensions among various clans of people, but for the most part, they all melded on the train, each behaving as though the person next to him was not in any way different from himself.

Public transportation, she thought. *The great equalizer.*

Then the spectacle of life around her was forgotten. It was familiar, after all. Instead, on the short train ride to Porter Square, Jenna found her mind drifting back to Damon, and wondering if things would be awkward with them tonight at dinner. It was almost like a double date, the four of them all hanging out together. Jenna had decided, however, that she wasn't going to handle it like that. Unless or until she and Damon started changing things on their own, she planned to make it fairly obvious that she thought they were all together as friends.

Whether it would stay that way was the real question.

When the train pulled into the station, it was a quarter past six. More than enough time for her to walk over to Professor Arora's house, return the books, and then make it back to Panda Garden before her friends got too hungry to wait for her. Jenna got off the train at Porter Square along with only a handful of other people who weren't headed for more exciting locations. She walked across the tiled floor and looked up in awe, as she always did, at the escalator. Porter Square was one of the deepest subway stations in the world, and the escalator seemed to go up and up forever.

It was sort of creepy, in a way, like being down inside a huge cave or something. But Jenna thought it was cool, too.

Up and up, she rode the escalator. A guy who'd gotten off the train behind her had dared to take the stairs. She'd seen others do the same thing, and had come to realize that there were some people who used those seemingly endless stairs as their daily exercise. From Jenna's perspective, exercise was one thing.

Masochism is something else entirely.

She was quite content with the escalator. As were most of the people who used Porter Square T Station.

When she reached the street, she immediately headed out onto Massachusetts Avenue toward Harvard Square. She remembered Nick's Beef and Beer as the major landmark that let her know which street was Professor Arora's—*How could I forget a place with that name? You've got to have testosterone just to say it correctly!*—and found it easily.

For a moment Jenna wasn't certain if Professor Arora's house was the fourth or fifth one on the left. Both were sort of dull, square-looking colonials. But then she remembered the little oak tree in the professor's yard and strode up the front walk to the door. There wasn't much light coming from inside, so she couldn't see past the narrow curtains that blocked the little windows on either side of the door. Jenna was carrying the two books in a plastic bag from Somerset Video, and she shifted it to her left hand to ring the bell.

She waited several seconds, but there was no answer. Feeling a bit foolish for not having called first, she knocked lightly on the door. For a moment, she thought she heard something. *Maybe the TV, or a radio playing,* Jenna reasoned. But then the sound was gone.

Still, nobody came to the door.

With a small sigh of surrender, Jenna looked

around for a place to stash the bag somewhere out of sight so the books would not be stolen, or damaged by bad weather. The storm door in front was locked, so she couldn't even leave the books inside that door. Jenna was beginning to wonder if the whole trip had been wasted. It would be frustrating to have to come back.

Still in search of somewhere to stash the books, so that she might leave Indira a message about it later, she started around the side of the house.

Damn. I look like a ghost.

Danny stood in the men's room just outside the detective squad room and surveyed his appearance in the mirror. He wasn't at all happy with what he saw, which was mainly the desperate need for some sleep and possibly just enough sun to make his complexion something besides corpse-pale. In the surreal fluorescent light, he did indeed look a bit ghostly.

Or maybe just haunted.

"Get me outta here," he mumbled, as he washed his hands. He used the excess water to dampen down the hair that jutted at an odd angle over his forehead, and headed out.

His mind was on the sloppy meatball subs he got so often from Dino's, just down the street from his apartment. One of those, dripping with melted mozzarella and provolone, and a couple of IBC root beers was his idea of bliss right about then. Of course, he'd have to combine those things with incessant, mindless channel-surfing and his sofa.

When Danny walked back into the squad room, he was smiling for the first time in hours. The smile lasted right up until he noticed Audrey. She was holding the phone against her ear with her shoulder, and scribbling something on a piece of paper.

"Come on," Danny said. "We're done, Audrey. Tell 'em nobody's home."

"Got it," she said into the phone. "Thanks." Then she hung up and looked at Danny. "Get your jacket, partner. We've got a DOA took a flier off an apartment house on Church Street. Looks like a domestic violence thing."

"Not a jumper?" Danny asked, frowning.

"Boyfriend says she jumped. Witnesses say he threw her."

Danny shook his head and sighed. "Yeah. That's how I usually solve my squabbles." He went to grab his jacket and saw Dwight Ross and Mike Cardiff walk into the squad room for the late shift.

"Evenin', Daniel," Dwight said gruffly. He was a big man with a thick white mustache and not much hair. The senior detective with Somerset P.D.

"Mariano," Cardiff muttered. He was gaunt and appeared older than he was. Mike Cardiff didn't talk much.

"Dwight. Mike. I don't think I've ever been happier to see a couple of grumpy old men in my life," Danny said.

"Let's go, Danny," Audrey said, starting past him with the piece of paper she'd written on.

Audrey had put up with a lot to get to the point she'd reached in her career. And a lot of what she'd put up with had come from Dwight and Mike. Danny knew she didn't like to ask for anything from them, but they were on the job too. It was their shift, their responsibility. Danny grabbed the white slip out of Audrey's hand and ignored her glare as he held it out to Dwight.

"You guys are running a little late, huh? Well, Audrey and I manned the phones for you. Took this call. You're on duty now, right?"

Dwight nodded, even smiled a little. "Yeah, Danny. We're catching. What, you got a hot date?"

"Only with the sandman."

He thanked them, and headed for the door, with Audrey following in silence. On the stairs, she mumbled something, and he turned to face her.

"What?"

"It was our case," she said. "Probably an easy collar. I figured you'd be happy for something simple after all this soul killer crap."

Danny frowned. "Yeah. Maybe we'll get another guy throwing his girlfriend off a roof in the morning," he said tiredly. "But it's their shift, now, Audrey. I just want to go home and give it a rest for a while."

Before she could answer, Cardiff appeared at the top of the stairs.

"Gaines," the man said flatly. "You got a call."

"Damn it!" Danny snapped. "Can't we just get out of here?"

"It's Joe Flannery," Cardiff added.

Danny and Audrey stared at each other with no expression. Then they turned and started back up the stairs, moving swiftly. The phone lay on its side on Audrey's desk, and she snatched it up fast, as though it might snap at her.

"Joe," she said. "What've you got?"

Impatient, Danny studied her face for some sign of what the news might be. A moment later he got it. Audrey smiled. Then she bent over the pad on her desk, and started writing. A moment later, she tore the sheet off the pad.

"Got it," she said. "We'll meet you there." Audrey hung up the phone and smiled grimly at Danny. "We've got her. I'll drive."

On the way down the stairs, he glanced at her. "So?"

"Cab driver saw her running out of Harvard yard to a car," Audrey said, fumbling for her keys. "She cut him off, which is why he remembered it. Got a make and model on the car, and a partial plate. First three letters happened to be his initials."

"Talk about coincidence," Danny said as they climbed into the car. "So was she on our list?"

Audrey handed him the slip of paper, then started up the car. Danny took it and stared at it a moment.

"You've got to be kidding."

Dr. Slikowski was reading a colleague's book about crime science when the phone rang. He thought the volume too heavy on crime and too light on science, likely for sensationalism and the sake of selling more copies, and he was glad to have a reason to put it down.

"Hello?"

"It's Danny Mariano, Doc. Sorry to disturb you at home, but I thought you'd want to know. Looks like we've got our killer. Audrey and I are in the car now, headed over there."

"Thank God," Slick said, almost more to himself than to Danny. "I appreciate your calling, Detective."

"The least we can do," Danny told him. "I'll give you a call in the morning, let you know how it shakes out."

"I'll look forward to it," the M.E. replied. "I'm sure Jenna will be relieved as well. Was she a student of Indira Arora's, then?"

When Danny answered, Slick's eyebrows shot up. Then he hung up with Danny and wheeled his chair over to the desk in his living room to look up Jenna's number. He dialed quickly, and glanced up at the clock as the phone on the other end of the line began to ring.

It was quarter to seven.

There was no answer.

Yoshiko stood in the open door to Sparrow 311, holding the knob, about to go back in to answer the phone.

"We're gonna be late," Hunter reminded her. "You told Jenna seven, right? Just let the machine get it."

"What if it's Jenna?" Damon suggested.

Yoshiko looked at Hunter, and he shrugged. She went into the room just as she heard the clicking of the answering machine picking up the call. Then she picked up the phone.

"Hello?"

"Who is it?" Hunter asked. He and Damon had come into the room behind her.

"They hung up," Yoshiko replied, and dropped the phone back into its cradle.

"I hate that," Damon said. "Just leave a message. That's what the machine's for, right?"

"They'll call back," Hunter said.

When she walked around the back of Professor Arora's house, Jenna noticed that there were lights on in the basement. *Maybe someone's home after all,* she thought. The plastic bag with the books was heavy, and the handle had started to tear, so she held it against her chest as she crouched to peer in through the filthy glass.

The basement was dusty cement. A clothesline was strung across her view, but she could see the washer and dryer and a lot of laundry. There was a stationary bike there as well. Jenna wasn't surprised. Indira was in pretty good shape. Past the clothesline, she could see the top and bottom of the stairs that came down from the first floor. For a moment she thought she saw someone moving beyond the stairs.

A quick glance around the yard revealed no obvious place for her to stash the books, other than just leave them on the stoop behind the back door.

I'll ring again, she thought. *Maybe she didn't hear me down in the basement.*

Just as she started around to the front of the house again, Jenna heard someone shriek in agony.

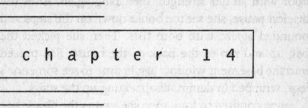

chapter 14

No!" cried the voice. "Please!"

She couldn't make out anything else amidst the crying and screaming, but it was coming from inside the house. From the basement.

Jenna ran back and peered in through the basement window, but she couldn't see anything. She knew she had to get help—the police, or even a neighbor. But as she ran around the front, holding the books tight against her, a terrible thought struck her.

Whoever that is, she could be dead before I get back. She stopped, glanced frantically around, and then studied the front of the house. *I can't just go back to the front door. Or could I?*

In her mind, she flashed back to the basement window. It was bigger than on more modern houses. Big enough, maybe.

Without another thought, Jenna ran up to the front

of the house and rang the bell. She pounded on the door with all her strength, then rang again. After the briefest pause, she set the books down on the steps and pounded again, with both fists. Then she picked the bag up and ran to the back of the house. She peered into the basement window just in time to see someone's legs, wrapped in denim, disappearing up the stairs.

Jenna counted to four, then she swung the plastic bag with the heavy books in it and shattered that basement window. It didn't make as much noise as she'd expected, and most of the glass landed inside on dirty laundry. But she knew, even as she used her heel to kick out the remaining shards of glass, that what she was doing was crazy.

The knowledge only made her work faster. Jenna slipped through the shattered window backward and dropped to the floor with a cut in her palm for her trouble. She heard the door close upstairs and knew that at the very least, her ruse at the door had been discovered. Shoving hanging laundry out of the way, Jenna stepped around the stairs to peer into the other side of the basement.

She was too late.

"Oh God, Indira," she whispered.

Professor Arora lay on the cement in a widening pool of blood, one dead eye wide and staring. Around her were a variety of symbols painted in white, and a haphazard collection of ritual trinkets, candles . . . a human skull. Indira's belly had been flayed open. There were at least a dozen visible stab wounds. One of her eyes had been cut out.

Jenna saw the knife.

Then the door to the basement opened.

Jenna was moving before she realized it. Her foot lashed out, kicking the knife away to slide under a metal utility shelf at the back of the basement. Jenna moved swiftly to the side of the stairs. The moment that same pair of denim-clad legs started down, she reached up and grabbed onto an ankle—and yanked.

Carol Westling fell headfirst down the stairs, slamming her shoulder into the edge of a wooden step as she tumbled end over end. The back of her head smacked the concrete, but not hard enough to do more than disorient her.

That was enough for Jenna. She didn't say a word as she leaped over the fallen woman, who swore loudly and reached for her. Jenna bolted up the stairs and into the kitchen. She could hear Carol's feet on the basement stairs as she ran for the front door. It took her a precious few seconds to get the chain lock off, and by the time she threw the door open, Carol was racing down the hall toward her. Jenna didn't know where she'd gotten it, but the woman had a taser in her hand, a little blue light buzzing between the contact points on its face.

"Jenna, wasn't it?" Carol said happily. "Your timing is perfect. When I saw the news, I thought Indira was my last chance. But now . . ."

Carol started coughing, then lunged. Jenna whipped the door open and slammed out through the storm door. As she went down the steps, she glanced back and saw Carol wiping blood from her lips. *Blood she coughed up*, Jenna thought. *So she really is dying.*

"Just not soon enough," she huffed, as she ran.

The killer gave chase. Jenna bent into a sprint across the street and out toward Massachusetts Avenue, with Carol in pursuit, the taser in her hand. Traffic buzzed by on Mass Ave, and Jenna practically leaped out in front of a car, waving her arms frantically. The guy behind the wheel of the Lexus only scowled at her and kept moving. Jenna thought he had even looked over at Carol, but he didn't even slow down.

Why would he? Just a couple of women in a catfight, right? Jenna started to worry. Carol didn't have a gun or a knife, she wasn't screaming, and how many people would notice the blood on her hands and her shirt, now that it was getting dark?

Behind her, Carol started coughing again, but she barely slowed down. Jenna ran across the street and started toward Porter Square. She passed shops, most of which were closed. Nick's was across the street. She realized now she should have gone in there, but it was too late. If she tried to run back, Carol would be on her.

It was ridiculous. She felt that acutely. Here she was in the middle of a major street, cars going by, being chased by an insane, dying woman who thought by killing Jenna, she could take her body. It was surreal. It was silly. But that didn't mean it wasn't happening.

Jenna ran past an open pizza joint, and a convenience store, but she was moving too fast now. Carol was hustling after her, and she had finally figured out what her destination was. She wanted a bit of a headstart, and a phone, and then she wanted to get out of there.

The hideous metal structures meant to be modern art that sat in front of the Porter Square T station loomed up ahead. Jenna ran as fast as she could, gaining distance. When she shoved open the heavy door to the station, there was no one else there. But the phones were there. One of them was missing its receiver, and only a metal tentacle hung down where the handset ought to have been. Jenna grabbed the other, dialed 911, and waited, panting, glancing over her shoulder at the doors for Carol.

"Nine-one-one emergency operator—"

"My name is Jenna Blake. I'm at Porter Square T station and a woman is trying to kill me. Please hurry!"

Carol was coming through the door. Jenna dropped the phone and ran toward the token booth. Behind the glass, a white-haired woman looked at her with profound suspicion.

Jenna had an idea.

"Help!" she screamed, glancing quickly back to see Carol running toward her. "Let me in! You've got to help me. She's going to kill me!"

The booth would lock from the inside. It would be impenetrable, at least to Carol. She'd be safe until the police got there.

"Now come on back, honey. Talk to your mother. We can deal with this," Carol said kindly, the taser nowhere in sight.

The older woman in the booth scowled at Jenna. "Maybe you oughta give your mom a break, dear," she said.

219

"No," Jenna said, angry and panicked. "You don't—"

"Jenna."

There was something cold in Carol's voice, and Jenna turned to see the woman coming toward her, hands out in supplication, looking for all the world like a woman whose heart had been broken by her recalcitrant daughter. If you didn't see the blood.

"Look at her!" Jenna shrieked at the woman behind the glass. "Look at that blood."

The old lady looked, for just a moment, like she was finally starting to realize what was happening.

"Honey," Carol said, and coughed up blood. "Don't do this to me. Haven't you hurt me enough?"

The old lady glared at Jenna.

"Oh God!" Jenna shouted at her. "Just call the police!"

Then she spun around and punched Carol in the side of the face, as hard as she could. The woman staggered, bent over, coughing, and then started after her again.

Jenna jumped the metal turnstiles and headed for the escalators and the stairs up ahead. For half a second, she thought about taking the stairs. She was afraid she might trip and fall on the escalators if she tried to run down them.

But then she was just doing it, her body moving faster than her mind. The steps of the escalator moved beneath her, and she reached out and grabbed hold of the huge rubber tracks on either side of her and started jumping down, three and four steps at a time.

She could hear Carol coughing behind her.

For someone who's dying, she moves pretty damn fast,

Jenna thought. Then something else hit her. Carol Westling figured Jenna was her last chance to survive.

We're both running for our lives.

"Flannery's already here," Audrey said as she took the turn, too fast, onto the street where Professor Arora lived with her roommate, Carol Westling.

The killer.

On top of the car, the bubble light flashed blue across trees and houses. Danny leaned forward a bit, studying the three police cars stopped on the narrow street ahead of them. There were two patrol cars and an unmarked—Flannery's. A uniformed cop stood on the front steps alone. As Audrey pulled the car up in front of the house, Danny unbuckled his seat belt and jumped out. He pulled out the little I.D. wallet in which he carried his badge, flipped it backward, and slipped it into his jacket pocket so the badge was displayed.

"What's going on?" he demanded of the uniform at the door.

"DOA inside," the cop replied. "Door was open, but the perp ain't around."

Audrey came up behind him, and Danny was about to push past the cop when Joe Flannery appeared inside the house with another detective and a pair of uniformed cops.

"You made good time," Flannery said grimly. "I wish we'd both been faster. Ten, fifteen minutes, Professor Arora would still be alive."

"Damn it!" Audrey snapped.

"Window broken in the back," Flannery went on. "Don't know why. Also no idea where the hell the Westling woman took off to."

"She could be anywhere," Danny said.

"She's not goin' far," Flannery replied. "We called her doctor. He didn't want to talk, but we didn't give him a choice. Can't have more than a month to live, if that."

Danny glanced at Audrey. "Let's have a look around."

As he turned to walk around the side of the house, Danny saw the driver's door of the closest patrol car open, and a uniformed officer jogged up toward the door.

"Detective Flannery," the officer said quickly. "Nine-one-one just got a call from Porter Square station. The Blake girl, the one who works for Dr. Slikowski? She said someone was trying to kill her."

Flannery swore. Danny didn't even take the time to do that. He was running toward the car, with Audrey beside him.

"How in hell does that girl always manage to get herself in the middle of stuff like this?" Audrey scowled.

"She's just naturally curious."

"It's gonna get her killed," Audrey snapped.

Danny didn't argue.

Jenna's chest hurt; her breathing came in ragged gasps. She had given up trying to go down multiple stairs at a time and was just moving down them as quickly as she was able. Behind her, Carol was coughing even more. At the top of the escalator, the old white-haired woman was shouting that she had called the police.

Thank God, Jenna thought. Even though she knew they couldn't get there in time.

"Hey!" shouted a man who was going up the escalator in the other direction. "Are you all right?"

"Do I look all right?" Jenna screamed back. "She's trying to kill me!"

The guy looked alarmed, took a quick glance at Carol, and then turned to try to come back down the escalator. It wasn't working, so he leaped over the side and onto the stairs, a bit of a drop below.

Jenna was amazed and hopeful. Finally someone had a little sense and a little guts. Someone was going to help.

She felt better.

She ran down the moving steps.

I'll be all right, she told herself. *That guy's going to help.*

Carol was coughing again behind her, trying to shout something at her. Jenna ignored her. She'd already put it together in her head, how the news of her illness must have driven the woman a little nuts, how she must have heard the stories of transmigration of the soul from Indira, and started researching.

Unless she really has done it before. The thought crossed Jenna's mind unbidden. She didn't want to consider that, but she couldn't help it. *What if it really is true?*

It didn't matter. Carol was still a killer.

Jenna was near the bottom of the escalator when Carol started coughing again and collapsed. She started tumbling down the escalator steps toward Jenna, shouting out in pain but clutching the taser tightly in her hand. Jenna leaped down a few steps, but the woman fell down toward her, so she jumped up on the sloping steel shelf that separated the escalator from the stairs beside them. The metal was slick, and the minute her body touched the surface, she started to slide. Round knobs of steel jutted up from it, and bruised her ribs and hips. She grunted in pain as she slid wildly down the metal divider on her stomach, feetfirst.

Then she was at the bottom, where she was dumped to the hard tiles. She looked up quickly to see Carol coming down after her again. The woman was bleeding now from the side of her face—*She must have hit one of the steps,* Jenna thought—but that wasn't stopping her.

Suddenly the guy from the escalator was next to her. "What the hell's going on?" he asked.

"She's gonna tell you she's my mother, but she's not!" Jenna said quickly, frantically, hoping he'd believe her. "She's trying to kill me!"

Jenna started backing up, into the station, looking for security guards. There was always a security guard down here, maybe more than one. And a cop sometimes, too. She'd seen them.

But now she didn't see anyone. Just a few people coming up the steps after getting off an outbound train on the level below. There was no one waiting for an inbound train, which meant one must have gone by only moments earlier. It would be at least a couple of minutes before another one came by.

Carol reached the bottom of the escalator.

"Lady, maybe you'd better just stay right there till a cop shows up. You got family trouble, you can sort it out then," the guy said.

"I told you, she's not my mother!" Jenna cried.

Then she turned and ran toward the platform, praying for an inbound train. She shouted at the passengers moving toward and past her, but they all gave her a wide berth, as if she were a crazy person or something.

Jenna turned just in time to see Carol bring the taser up and press it against the neck of the guy who had tried to help her. The guy groaned and collapsed to the tiles. A couple of commuters shouted at Carol and started toward her.

"Keep the hell away from me!" she screamed, tears slipping down her cheeks. "This is none of your god-damn business! It's a matter of life and death!"

Yeah, Jenna thought. *It is.*

With her tears and her raving and the blood soaking her shirt, nobody wanted to go anywhere near Carol. She looked at Jenna from fifty feet away and grinned.

"Don't you get it?" she asked. "I can do anything I want. Once I'm inside you, nobody can touch me for it. I mean, they're not going to punish you for my crimes, are they?"

Jenna backed up toward the edge of the platform.

Deep in the tunnel, she heard the squealing of a train twisting along the tracks.

Carol came at her at a run.

"Hey, get away from her!" yelled an older guy in a business suit.

He grabbed Carol's arm and she spun on him and

broke his nose. She kicked him between the legs, and when he bent over to clutch at his groin, she brought her knee up in his face. She left him there on the ground amidst the spit and the stubbed out cigarettes and kept on after Jenna.

Carol started to sing. Jenna was taken aback as she realized that the words were not in English. They sounded very foreign to her, and Jenna thought of the god Shiva, and the death dancing, and wondered if it was Hindi.

Carol started to dance a little as she approached, just a little jig one way and then the other. She held the taser up, ten feet away. Jenna was backed up to the edge of the platform, trapped.

Eight feet away.

Jenna darted to her right, running up the platform. There were maybe four or five people in that direction, but they cleared out of her way, shouting at Carol but not wanting to get too close. Carol ran after her, breathing hard, gasping, blood starting to drip from her nose.

Her mind awhirl, Jenna did the only thing she could think of. As Carol reached for her, Jenna dropped to her knees and bent over. Carol tried to jump over her, but failed. She stumbled over Jenna and fell over the edge of the platform onto the tracks.

The train was coming in fast. Jenna could see the lights in the tunnel. She stood up and looked over the edge of the platform. Carol's left leg was at an odd angle; it looked broken. The taser was gone, dropped somewhere on the tracks.

"Get up!" Jenna shouted at her. "The train!"

Carol smiled. "I'm dying anyway," she said.

Jenna was sorely tempted to leave her there, but she just couldn't. If she did nothing, she'd carry that guilt all her life. But she also wasn't an idiot. The train had rounded a curve in the tunnel and was barreling into the station.

"Get up here, damn you! Maybe you'll die, but it doesn't have to be today! You wanted more life, this is it!"

Snarling with the pain, Carol pushed herself up to stand on her right leg and then grabbed hold of the edge of the platform. Jenna helped drag her onto the tiled surface, brought her up to stand face-to-face with her.

"Good-bye, you stupid bitch," Carol grunted, and grabbed hold of Jenna, ready to push her in front of the train.

Fingers twined in Carol's hair and yanked her head back. Danny pulled Jenna out of the way as Audrey Gaines held her service weapon to Carol's temple and smiled.

"Watch who you're calling names," Audrey said.

Danny looked at Jenna, breathing hard from having run down into the station. "You okay?"

Jenna nodded, also panting.

Then Danny's expression changed. His eyes went hard as he whipped out a pair of handcuffs and walked around behind Carol Westling. He pulled her hands behind her back.

"You have the right to remain silent," he began.

Audrey glanced at Jenna.

"Girl," she said, "you have both the worst and the best luck I have ever seen."

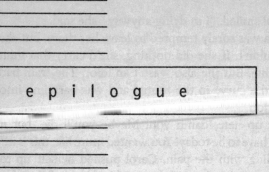

e p i l o g u e

Late Saturday morning Jenna stood on the roof of the library and stared out at the Boston skyline on the horizon. It was a perfectly clear day, and warmer than it had been in more than a week. She was comfortable in a navy blue Somerset sweatshirt and jeans. And she was quiet.

Jenna had been quiet much of the time since Thursday night.

"Do you ever wonder?" she asked, her voice low, a bit nervous.

"Wonder what?" Danny replied.

Her eyes unfocused, her thoughts turned inward, she turned to Danny but barely saw him.

"If it's possible," she explained, "that your soul could move, I mean. From one body to another."

He shifted uncomfortably, and several seconds passed before he replied. "If it is," he said at length, "I don't think it's something that can be forced. The story Professor Arora told, about the brain-damaged girl and the woman who supposedly lived again in her body? That's a story about somebody getting a second chance, and I don't think people like Carol Westling get a second chance."

That's pretty grim, Jenna thought. But then she remembered what Indira's body had looked like, and realized that maybe it wasn't so grim after all.

"Did you guys ever find out where she got those ashes?" Jenna asked.

"She wouldn't say," Danny revealed. "Gotta figure she stole them from somewhere, or had a relative who was cremated at some point. Or, if we buy your theory, maybe they were hers, from the first time around."

Jenna felt a little sick at the thought, and gave Danny an admonishing look.

"Hey, it was your idea," he protested.

"So how long does she have?" Jenna asked.

"A few weeks, maybe. She'll die before she ever sees trial."

Jenna frowned. "It must be terrible. Knowing when you're going to die. I don't know if I could deal with that."

Danny sort of chuckled, and Jenna looked more closely at him, focusing at last. He glanced away, a small smile on his face.

"*That's* funny?" she asked, incredulous.

"I thought maybe you meant did I wonder about us?" he admitted.

Jenna was surprised by his candor. He answered her next question before she could even ask it.

"I do. But that's all. I hope you can understand that. I think you're something else, Jenna. I'm glad to know you. But . . ."

"But nothing," Jenna said. "I do understand, Danny. Really. And it's okay. I'm just sorry if I embarrassed you. I never meant for that to happen."

"No regrets," he promised.

Several moments passed in silence as they looked out at the skyline together. A breeze blew across the library roof and Jenna shivered. Danny didn't put his arm around her, and that was good. She still had a crush on him, but Jenna wanted to make sure things stayed clear between her and Danny.

"No regrets," she said.

Monday, after her international relations class let out, Jenna went back to her dorm and waited for her roommate. When Yoshiko came in, the two of them walked over to the medical center together.

"Any message from your parents today?" Yoshiko asked.

"No, thank God. I guess they decided to give me the day off."

"They're just afraid for you."

Jenna laughed and shook her head. "*I'm* afraid for me."

"You and Damon still planning to go out this week?" Yoshiko asked, with a suggestive smile.

"I think so." Jenna nodded. "I didn't really before, but I'm starting to feel kind of *comfortable* with him. That's a nice thing to have. Damon's just what he seems to be, and I'm starting to find that pretty irresistible. So we'll see."

By that time they were riding up the elevator. When it opened on the second floor, and they stepped off, Jenna paused before heading down the hallway to Slick's office.

"You sure you want to do this?" Yoshiko asked.

"Not at all," Jenna confessed, and smiled thinly. "But I can't put it off forever."

Yoshiko walked beside her to the door, but Jenna went in alone. When she stepped inside, Dyson looked up immediately and smiled, truly happy to see her. Jenna could hear soft but funky jazz coming from Slick's inner office—Dave Grusin, she thought. Maybe the soundtrack from *The Fabulous Baker Boys*. Slick loved that one.

"Hey!" Dyson said and came over to wrap her in a tight embrace. "Jenna, I'm so glad to see you. We were both a little freaked when we heard what happened."

"Dr. Slikowski called me Friday," she said numbly. "To check up. I guess I wasn't much of a conversationalist."

"I don't blame you," Dyson said. "I'm gonna have to chain you to your desk. With your track record, that's about the only way we can keep you out of trouble."

Jenna offered a half smile and looked up to see Slick sitting in his wheelchair in the open door to his office.

He looked pained, as though just seeing her upset him. He looked like he cared very much.

"Are you all right?" he asked. "Truly?"

She took a deep breath, and nodded. "I will be, I think. Just a little shell-shocked. It's all been a little bit too much."

"Of course it has," Slick agreed. "You take your time, Jenna. Don't come back until you're ready."

Jenna glanced away, feeling a bit sick to her stomach. "That's what I came to tell you," she said, and then lifted her eyes to meet his gaze.

"I'm not coming back."

Turn the page for
a preview of
the next
Body of Evidence thriller

MEETS THE EYE

Available February 2000

Turn the page for

a look at

the next

Body of Evidence thriller

MEETS THE EYE

Available February 2000

The dead don't scare me," Jenna Blake said. "That's not what it's about."

On the other side of the dining room table, which was laden with a lavish Thanksgiving Day meal, her mother looked dubious. Before April Blake could question her daughter's words, Jenna went on.

"It's true," she said. "I don't get any of those creepy feelings in the autopsy room. Even being at the scene of a murder or an accident doesn't really bother me. Sure, it's nasty, and it's sad—on a scale of one to yuck it's up there. But none of that bothers me."

Jenna glanced at Yoshiko Kitsuta, her roommate at Somerset University, whom she'd brought home to share Thanksgiving at the Blakes's, since Yoshiko had decided not to fly home to Hawaii for just the weekend.

Yoshiko smiled. "Which is what makes you weird," she told Jenna. "If somebody wanted me to hold fresh human organs in my hands, I'd either faint or throw up."

Jenna shrugged. "Doesn't bother me."

"Which is wonderful," her mother said. "You used to be horrified by the sight of blood. You're over that. Maybe you could think about surgery, if you're not interested in going back to pathology."

"I didn't say that." Jenna looked away.

"But you *did* quit," April reminded her.

Jenna didn't have an immediate response to that. Her mother was right. She'd been working as a diener, or pathology assistant, at Somerset Medical Center, and loving every minute of it. Puzzles had always intrigued her, and she was enthralled by the idea of solving the puzzles that each autopsy represented, all while bringing peace of mind to the relatives of the deceased. But she had a tendency toward the more forensic end of pathology, toward figuring out not only what had happened, but why and how. Several times, it had put her in harm's way.

"It wasn't just that I was afraid," Jenna said, glancing away. "It wasn't just the danger."

April offered a slight shrug. "Well, you won't get any argument from me, honey. I'm just relieved you're out of there. If Dr. Slikowski were your average medical examiner, I wouldn't worry so much. But he gets too involved in these cases. It isn't safe." She stood up and smiled at the two girls. "So, who's for apple pie à la mode?"

Both Jenna and Yoshiko agreed that pie was very necessary. After April had gone into the kitchen, though, Yoshiko looked at Jenna with concern.

"You're waffling," Yoshiko observed. "It's spooking her. You said you weren't going back."

"I'm not," Jenna said, but even she didn't think it sounded convincing, So she said it more firmly. "I'm not."

That's a little better, she thought.

Yoshiko studied her a moment. "So, if it doesn't bother you hanging around dead people, and the danger isn't enough to scare you off, what is it?"

Jenna took a long breath and let it out, contemplating Yoshiko's question. It was the very thing she'd been grappling with in the weeks since she'd quit her job. Even on the drive home to Natick the previous night, her mind hadn't been on the road, or Thanksgiving, or the perfect fall evening, with the smell of wood burning in fireplaces that permeated the air when she got out of the car in front of her mother's house. She and Yoshiko didn't even talk that much on the drive out, though she'd been a little better today.

Can you say preoccupied?

Jenna smiled and looked at Yoshiko, who was waiting for an answer.

"I guess it's the insanity," she said at length. "The twisted, sick minds of the people who do this stuff. Maybe they're nuts or maybe they're evil or maybe they're just born without whatever it is that makes the rest of us human, but it makes me sick, Yosh. It's not even that it terrifies me as much as it makes me feel filthy, like I should be ashamed that I'm part of a species that can turn out monsters like that.

"I just got tired of feeling that way," Jenna said sadly.

"Wow," Yoshiko said softly. "I don't blame you. On the other hand, I've got to say you still don't sound one hundred percent, y'know?"

Jenna thought about it, her mind straying from the danger and the horror to the good she'd done as part of Slick's team. Their work had helped to stop at least two killers. She might even have saved lives by working to solve those mysteries. She . . .

No.

"I'm not going back," Jenna said firmly.

Jason Castillo had been working Boston P.D.'s narcotics division for seven years. In that time, he'd sat waiting for a drug deal to go down almost more often than he'd sat at his dinner table to eat. He was thirty-three, divorced, no children. His life was the job. The job was fishing.

That's how Castillo looked at it, anyway. Cast out the line, hook a little fish, maybe give it some play, let it run until it became bait for the big one, the real score. Right up the food chain. In that seven years, he'd seen all kinds of ways it could go down. Maybe the buy wouldn't happen, the deal would be off. Maybe it'd go down smooth and they'd send a couple of scumbags to jail. Two years ago, Castillo had his biggest bust, more than a thousand pounds of heroin on a boat in Boston Harbor. He'd made the news for that one.

Yeah, it was nice when it all went according to plan.

Sometimes, though, all hell would break loose, and things would get very, very messy.

But in seven years, Jason Castillo had never seen anything like this.

In an alley across the street, a bunch of gangbangers calling themselves the Dorchester Kings were about to hand over a bag full of cash for a suitcase loaded with enough swag to net a quarter of a million dollars on the street. It was the deal they thought would put them in the big time. But the Kings didn't know they had a mole. Boston P.D. had a man inside, wired for sound.

Greg Tarver was new to the narcotics division, but this bust was going to give him a solid start, no doubt. Not just the Kings, but the courier who brought the swag and made the switch. The idea was to get the courier to give up his boss, Anthony "Ant" Micellatti. Ant ran an import and export business, but it was pretty clear to the cops that he specialized in the import end of things.

So that was the setup. Castillo sat in a coffee shop across the street from the alley with a wire trailing up to the receiver in his ear. The other cops in his unit were spread out, ready to take the entire deal apart. Three of them were in a van half a block away, listening very carefully to what was going down. Two more in a car, pretending at a lovers' quarrel. Pete Karasiotis was digging through garbage bins for returnable cans and bottles. And Castillo sipped his coffee and watched the Dorchester Kings roll on up in their rumbling, barely street-legal rides.

They spilled out of the two cars, leaving the drivers behind, ready to go. Five guys went into the alley, glancing around, looking for trouble. Castillo sipped his coffee and waited right along with them. None of them had long to wait. Barely three minutes after the Kings entered the alley, the courier appeared, walking at a steady clip along the sidewalk, a heavy suitcase in his hand.

"Christ, these guys are fearless," Castillo muttered to himself. *That's what they think of our legal system,* he thought. *Take a bust, and my lawyer has me out in time for breakfast.*

"Not this time," he whispered over the rim of his coffee cup.

In his ear, he could hear the conversation begin, thanks to Tarver's wire. The bluster, the bullshit male posturing. The Kings tested the merchandise, and then the courier zipped his suitcase again. They started to make the trade.

Castillo grabbed the walkie-talkie clipped to his belt. "Do it," he barked.

But even as he headed for the door, something went terribly wrong. He heard shouting, threats. Someone had come into the alley who wasn't supposed to be there. Castillo's first thought was that it was a civilian, stumbling into the wrong place at the wrong time. A civilian who was about to die. Then the gunfire started.

With a curse, he pushed out the door of the coffee

shop, unclipped his service weapon from its holster, and bolted across the street toward the alley. Pete Karasiotis met him halfway.

"What the hell—" Castillo started.

"Someone else showed up. Solo!" Karasiotis blurted in astonishment. "Guy just went in and opened fire."

Castillo thought the other cop had more to say, but then a bullet punched through Karasiotis's skull at the temple, and the man went down in a bloody sprawl on the street.

He didn't have time to report in. It didn't matter anyway. He knew the others would be coming in. Even now, the rest of the unit was moving on his position. It would only be seconds before they arrived.

Castillo didn't have seconds.

At the mouth of the alley stood a man dressed in a rumpled, blood-spattered suit. He had the suitcase full of swag and the bag of cash clutched in his right hand, and a gun in the other. Apparently one dead cop wasn't enough for him, because he opened fire even as Castillo aimed his own weapon.

The hollow pop of gunfire thudded dully from the blind faces of gray buildings. A bullet punched through Castillo's shoulder, hard enough to spin him sideways. In shock, wound burning, bleeding, he went down. He tried to lift his weapon, to take aim, but the guy was above him then.

The shooter's face was white and pale and expressionless, like he was bored, or about to fall asleep. His eyes barely registered Castillo, or anything else for that matter. He looked almost dead as he pointed the gun at Castillo's forehead.

Gunfire ripped through the night again, and the shooter jittered, dropping what he'd stolen as bullets punctured his chest and abdomen and leg. He crumpled to the ground next to Castillo, and the cop sat up, one hand on his wound and the other holding his weapon steady, waiting to see if the guy would rise.

The shooter never got up. He bled out there on the street, not far from the load of money and heroin he'd killed for, and died for. Castillo gritted his teeth with the pain in his shoulder, and stared in mute fury at the dead man.

"Ain't this a fiasco?" muttered Ned Schulman, as he came up behind Castillo. "Ambulance is on the way, Jace. The skels driving for the Kings took off as soon as the shooting started. What the hell happened?"

Castillo shook his head, trying to make sense of it. The shooter must have been working solo, but nobody was that crazy. Even if you knew the deal was going down, even if you could kill a bunch of gangbangers and drug dealers and walk away with the profits, no way would it go unavenged. The guy had to have been nuts.

He looked nuts, that was for sure. *Or something.* All Castillo knew was that all of his suspects and two good cops were dead, and he had no idea why.

"God, Jace, did you take a look at this guy?" Schulman asked, shocked.

Castillo frowned, having a hard time focusing on anything but the wound in his shoulder and the sound of the siren from the approaching ambulance. But he managed to turn and look at the shooter's face.

"You know him?" Castillo asked.

"*You* know him," Schulman insisted. "It's that reporter. Harrigan."

"What? From the *Globe?*"

"That's him."

Incredulous, Castillo took a closer look. He hadn't seen Sean Harrigan in person in a couple of years, but it looked like Schulman was right.

Which was impossible.

"Can't be," Castillo said. "Harrigan's been dead almost a month. Heart attack."

"Yeah? Then tell me who this is, then."

But Jason Castillo didn't have an answer for that.

Look for the next
Body of Evidence **thriller**
MEETS THE EYE
by
Christopher Golden
Available from Pocket Pulse
February 2000

about the author

CHRISTOPHER GOLDEN is the award-winning, *L.A. Times*–bestselling author of such novels as *Strangewood* and the three-volume *Shadow Saga; Hellboy: The Lost Army;* and the Body of Evidence series of teen thrillers (including *Thief of Hearts* and *Soul Survivor*), which is currently being developed for television.

He has also written or cowritten a great many books, both novels and nonfiction, based on the popular TV series *Buffy the Vampire Slayer.*

Golden's comic-book work includes the recent *Wolverine/Punisher: Revelation* and stints on *The Crow* and *Spider-Man Unlimited.* Upcoming projects include a run on *Buffy the Vampire Slayer; Batman: Real Worlds* for DC; and the ongoing monthly *Angel* series, tying into the *Buffy* television spinoff.

The editor of the Bram Stoker Award–winning book of criticism *CUT!: Horror Writers on Horror Film,* he has written articles for the *Boston Herald, Disney Adventures* and *Billboard,* among others, and was a regular columnist for the worldwide service BPI Entertainment News Wire.

Before becoming a full-time writer, he was licensing manager for *Billboard* magazine in New York, where he worked on Fox Television's *Billboard Music Awards* and *American Top 40* radio, among many other projects.

Golden was born and raised in Massachusetts, where he still lives with his family. He graduated from Tufts University. He is currently at work on his next novel, *Straight On 'til Morning*. Please visit him at www.christophergolden.com.

Bullying.
Threats.
Bullets.

Locker searches? Metal detectors?

Fight back without fists.

. . . A GIRL BORN
WITHOUT THE FEAR GENE

FEARLESS™

A NEW SERIES BY
FRANCINE PASCAL

A TITLE AVAILABLE EVERY MONTH

From Pocket Pulse
Published by Pocket Books

BUFFY

THE VAMPIRE

SLAYER™

IMMORTAL

She cannot die.
Strike her down, but like the night she will always
come again.
And she will bring forth the end of Man....

Has Buffy met her match in an
immortal vampire?

The first Buffy hardcover
by Christopher Golden and Nancy Holder

Available from Pocket Books

2310